TOEIC

練習測驗（1）

LISTENING TEST

In the Listening test, you will be asked to demonstrate how well you understand spoken English. The entire Listening test will last approximately 45 minutes. There are four parts, and directions are given for each part. You must mark your answers on the separate answer sheet. Do not write your answers in your test book.

PART 1

Directions: For each question in this part, you will hear four statements about a picture in your test book. When you hear the statements, you must select the one statement that best describes what you see in the picture. Then find the number of the question on your answer sheet and mark your answer. The statements will not be printed in your test book and will be spoken only one time.

Statement (C), "They're sitting at a table," is the best description of the picture, so you should select answer (C) and mark it on your answer sheet.

1.

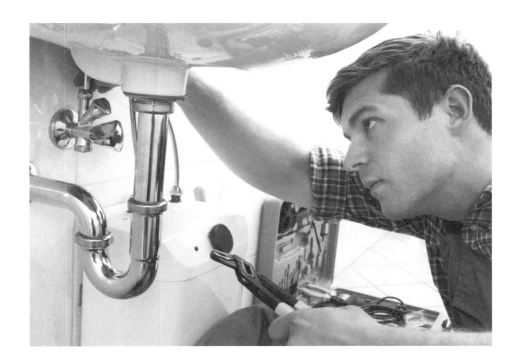

2.

GO ON TO THE NEXT PAGE

3.

4.

5.

6.

GO ON TO THE NEXT PAGE

PART 2

7. Mark your answer on your answer sheet.

8. Mark your answer on your answer sheet.

9. Mark your answer on your answer sheet.

10. Mark your answer on your answer sheet.

11. Mark your answer on your answer sheet.

12. Mark your answer on your answer sheet.

13. Mark your answer on your answer sheet.

14. Mark your answer on your answer sheet.

15. Mark your answer on your answer sheet.

16. Mark your answer on your answer sheet.

17. Mark your answer on your answer sheet.

18. Mark your answer on your answer sheet.

19. Mark your answer on your answer sheet.

20. Mark your answer on your answer sheet.

21. Mark your answer on your answer sheet.

22. Mark your answer on your answer sheet.

23. Mark your answer on your answer sheet.

24. Mark your answer on your answer sheet.

25. Mark your answer on your answer sheet.

26. Mark your answer on your answer sheet.

27. Mark your answer on your answer sheet.

28. Mark your answer on your answer sheet.

29. Mark your answer on your answer sheet.

30. Mark your answer on your answer sheet.

31. Mark your answer on your answer sheet.

Directions: You will hear some conversations between two people. You will be asked to answer three questions about what the speakers say in each conversation. Select the best response to each question and mark the letter (A), (B), (C), or (D) on your answer sheet. The conversation will not be printed in your test book and will be spoken only one time.

32. What is the woman asking about?
(A) A refund.
(B) A job.
(C) A repair.
(D) A sale.

33. Why does the man apologize?
(A) An item is out of stock.
(B) An employee is not available.
(C) A store policy has changed.
(D) A fee is charged for a service.

34. What does the woman say she will do in the afternoon?
(A) Return to the shop.
(B) Submit an application.
(C) Confirm a payment.
(D) Call a vendor.

35. Why did the man come to the print shop?
(A) To inquire about a discount.
(B) To pick up an order.
(C) To complain about a service.
(D) To request express delivery.

36. What does the woman say about the account?
(A) It is registered under the company name.
(B) It has not been activated.
(C) It is missing an address.
(D) It is eligible for an upgrade.

37. Why does the man say, "That's going to be a problem"?
(A) He lost his credit card.
(B) He doesn't have the invoice.
(C) He forgot his ID.
(D) He doesn't like the sticker design.

38. Where are the speakers most likely to be?
(A) At a car dealership.
(B) At a utility company office.
(C) At an appliance store.
(D) At a garden center.

39. What does the woman want to talk to a manager about?
(A) Long waiting times.
(B) A misleading advertisement.
(C) A helpful employee.
(D) High-quality merchandise.

40. What will the man do next?
(A) Return at another time.
(B) Visit a website.
(C) Contact his manager.
(D) Read a manual.

41. Who, most likely, is Woman A?
(A) A restaurant cook.
(B) An architect.
(C) A financial adviser.
(D) A flower shop owner.

42. What are the Lamberts considering doing?
(A) Leasing out their apartment.
(B) Expanding their business.
(C) Opening a bank account.
(D) Changing his profession.

43. What does the man ask Woman B to do?
(A) Prepare a report.
(B) Order some equipment.
(C) Create a design.
(D) Sign a contract.

GO ON TO THE NEXT PAGE.

44. Where does the conversation most likely take place?
- (A) At a concert hall.
- (B) At a photography studio.
- (C) At a toy store.
- (D) At a museum.

45. According to the man, what has recently changed?
- (A) An entrance fee has increased.
- (B) Memberships are now available.
- (C) An exhibit has been relocated.
- (D) A building addition has been completed.

46. Why does the man encourage the woman to hurry?
- (A) An event is expected to be crowded.
- (B) A video is about to begin.
- (C) A building is closing soon.
- (D) Supplies are limited.

---

47. Where are the speakers?
- (A) At a sales conference.
- (B) At a real estate seminar.
- (C) At an open auction.
- (D) At a graduation ceremony.

48. What does the woman say makes her successful?
- (A) Her ability to handle multiple projects.
- (B) Her organizational skills.
- (C) Her international experience.
- (D) Her knowledge of the area.

49. What advice does Man B/Mr. Fielding give?
- (A) Set personal goals at the start of projects.
- (B) Build relationships with clients.
- (C) Stay up to date on industry trends.
- (D) Collaborate with other departments.

---

50. What does the woman want to do?
- (A) Make a payment.
- (B) Claim a package.
- (C) Check in to a hotel.
- (D) Visit a friend.

51. What is the most likely reason that the woman's name is missing from the list?
- (A) She is a new resident.
- (B) She is a former employee.
- (C) Her subscription was not renewed.
- (D) Her name was misspelled.

52. What does the man initially ask for?
- (A) An identification card.
- (B) A contract.
- (C) An e-mail address.
- (D) A contact name.

---

53. Who is the man most likely to be?
- (A) An author.
- (B) An accountant.
- (C) A librarian.
- (D) A bank clerk.

54. What does the man offer to do?
- (A) Sign a form.
- (B) Obtain a book.
- (C) Create an account.
- (D) Copy a document.

55. Why will the woman be charged a fee?
- (A) For canceling a reservation.
- (B) For renewing a membership.
- (C) For using a special service.
- (D) For replacing a lost card.

Internships Available at Universal Media

Accounting and Finance
Public Relations
Art and Design
Staging and Lighting
Post-Production

56. What does the woman want to do?
(A) Make an airline reservation.
(B) Renew a driver's license.
(C) Apply for a research grant.
(D) Obtain a passport.

57. What does the woman inquire about?
(A) Citizenship.
(B) Airfares.
(C) Expedited service.
(D) Travel times.

58. Look at the graphic. Which of the following is NOT required for a first-time passport?
(A) An original birth certificate.
(B) Proof of identity.
(C) Four photographs.
(D) A 60 dollar fee.

59. Where does the woman work?
(A) At a university.
(B) At a television station.
(C) At a public library.
(D) At a media company.

60. How does the woman know Oliver Brown?
(A) He recently submitted a resume.
(B) He is a local celebrity.
(C) They are making a film together.
(D) They used to work at the same company.

61. Look at the graphic. Which internship would the man most likely be interested in?
(A) Accounting and Finance.
(B) Public Relations.
(C) Art and Design.
(D) Staging and Lighting.

GO ON TO THE NEXT PAGE.

SERVICE DIRECTORY	
Front Desk	0
Housekeeping	110
Room Service	112
Concierge	114
Gift Shop	116

NEW SCHEDULE BEGINNING WEEK OF AUGUST 3	
Tom K. (manager)	7:30 a.m.– 5:30 p.m.
Pete L.	9:00 a.m.– 7:00 p.m.
Lydia O.	10:30 a.m.– 8:30 p.m.
Kevin J.	12:00 p.m.–10:00 p.m.

62. Where does the woman most likely work?
(A) At a movie theater.
(B) At a restaurant.
(C) At a hotel.
(D) At an architectural firm.

63. What is causing a problem?
(A) Noise from construction work.
(B) A shortage of trained staff.
(C) A delayed opening.
(D) An incorrect bill.

64. Look at the graphic. What number will the man probably call?
(A) 110.
(B) 112.
(C) 114.
(D) 116.

65. Who is the woman most likely to be?
(A) A hotel manager.
(B) A tour operator.
(C) A music instructor.
(D) A flight attendant.

66. What is the man concerned about?
(A) The size of some rooms.
(B) An extra storage fee.
(C) Some travel connections.
(D) The safe transport of instruments.

67. What does the woman suggest?
(A) Purchasing additional tickets.
(B) Talking to a security guard.
(C) Contacting the vendor directly.
(D) Making a detailed schedule.

68. Look at the graphic. According to the new schedule, what time will the man get off work?
(A) 5:30 p.m.
(B) 7:00 p.m.
(C) 8:30 p.m.
(D) 10:00 p.m.

69. What does the woman recommend?
(A) Taking a different route.
(B) Reviewing some documents.
(C) Biking to work.
(D) Making copies.

70. Why did the man miss the meeting?
(A) He had another appointment.
(B) He woke up late.
(C) He was caught in traffic.
(D) He was preparing a presentation.

Directions: You will hear some talks given by a single speaker. You will be asked to answer three questions about what the speaker says in each talk. Select the best response to each question and mark the letter (A), (B), (C), or (D) on your answer sheet. The talks will not be printed in your test book and will be spoken only one time.

71. What bothers the woman about Indus Outsourcing?
    (A) Their request to revise a contract.
    (B) Their focus on cost cutting.
    (C) Their failure to meet deadlines.
    (D) Their problems with staffing.

72. What does the woman mean when she says, "Here's the deal"?
    (A) She has found what she was looking for.
    (B) She will introduce a point to consider.
    (C) She will demonstrate a product.
    (D) She has forgotten a word.

73. What are the listeners asked to look at?
    (A) A list of agencies.
    (B) A business report.
    (C) An advertisement.
    (D) A travel itinerary.

---

74. Where does the announcement take place?
    (A) In a café.
    (B) In a hardware store.
    (C) On a ferryboat.
    (D) On an airplane.

75. What is the main topic of this announcement?
    (A) A change in a schedule.
    (B) Weekly specials.
    (C) An item that has just been found.
    (D) A service that was recently introduced.

76. What will most likely happen next?
    (A) A policy will be updated.
    (B) A video will be shown.
    (C) A group will be seated.
    (D) A price will be reduced.

---

77. Who are the listeners most likely to be?
    (A) Game developers.
    (B) Mail clerks.
    (C) Hotel staff.
    (D) Restaurant managers.

78. What will the listeners do at the workshop?
    (A) Learn to use new software.
    (B) Develop goals for the upcoming year.
    (C) Discuss customer feedback.
    (D) Participate in role-playing activities.

79. What does the speaker expect will happen?
    (A) There will be fewer billing errors.
    (B) Employees will work more efficiently.
    (C) Customers will write positive reviews.
    (D) Sales will increase.

---

80. What type of business is being advertised?
    (A) A clothing shop.
    (B) A hair salon.
    (C) A travel agency.
    (D) A computer store.

81. According to the speaker, what will be available this week?
    (A) A free class.
    (B) Longer hours.
    (C) A new location.
    (D) A 50 percent discount.

82. Why does the speaker suggest listeners visit Web site?
    (A) To sign up for the mailing list.
    (B) To read customer reviews.
    (C) To request technical help.
    (D) To make an appointment.

GO ON TO THE NEXT PAGE

83. What is being advertised?
- (A) A publishing company.
- (B) A job placement agency.
- (C) A law firm.
- (D) A business school.

84. What advantage does the speaker mention?
- (A) An online consultation.
- (B) A driving certificate.
- (C) Discounted membership.
- (D) Free legal advice.

85. Please look at the graphic. What is required to access an online consultant?
- (A) A current driver's license.
- (B) An email address.
- (C) A verification code.
- (D) A cell phone number.

---

86. Why are the people meeting?
- (A) To discuss a festival change.
- (B) To watch a selection of films.
- (C) To greet some international visitors.
- (D) To vote for a new board member.

87. What needs to be added to the schedule?
- (A) A keynote speaker.
- (B) A banquet location.
- (C) Another music category.
- (D) Actors' interviews.

88. Why does the man say, "This is not up to me"?
- (A) He took part in the discussion.
- (B) He prefers international music.
- (C) He suggested they include more variety.
- (D) He may not agree with the idea.

89. Look at the graphic. When did Janet Rossi place the call to Steve Gunt?
- (A) On Monday.
- (B) On Tuesday.
- (C) On Wednesday.
- (D) On Thursday.

90. According to the speaker, what has not changed?
- (A) The workshop topic.
- (B) The project budget.
- (C) The sales goal.
- (D) The meeting location.

91. Who, most likely, is the message for?
- (A) A computer technician.
- (B) A project manager.
- (C) An accountant.
- (D) A sales clerk.

CITY OF DAYTON
TOWN HALL MEETING AGENDA
July 12 at 7:00 p.m.

7:00-7:10   Welcome and introduction   Joe O'Brien, moderator

• Purpose of meeting – Olivia Collins, City of Dayton mayor
• City of Dayton, Office of Budget and Management – Ivan Portensky, city budget director
• Montgomery County Commissioner's Office – Scott Favreau, acting deputy

8:30-9:30   Public comment and open discussion – Joe O'Brien, moderator

---

UNIVERSAL SOLUTIONS
1234 Delaware Ave., Washington, D.C.
"Branding is our business"

Lucy Gonzales
Senior Media Analyst

Contact: (708) 340-2222 office
Email: l_gonzales@globaloutreach.com

---

92. Look at the graphic. Who is the current speaker?
(A) Joe O'Brien.
(B) Olivia Collins.
(C) Ivan Portensky.
(D) Scott Favreau.

93. What did the city do in June?
(A) Initiate a temporary program.
(B) Change parking regulations.
(C) Hold an election.
(D) Fire three police officers.

94. What problem is the speaker addressing?
(A) Scheduling delays.
(B) Road congestion.
(C) Budget reductions.
(D) Street repairs.

---

95. What public event does the speaker describe?
(A) A sports competition.
(B) A musical concert.
(C) A cooking demonstration.
(D) An art contest.

96. What will the radio station offer for free?
(A) T-shirts.
(B) Wall calendars.
(C) Food and beverages.
(D) Upcoming event tickets.

97. According to the speaker, what will be broadcast next?
(A) An advertisement.
(B) A live interview.
(C) A weather forecast.
(D) A music performance.

---

98. What does the speaker want to do?
(A) Hire a designer.
(B) Change an order.
(C) Preview an agenda.
(D) Paint a wall.

99. What problem does the speaker mention?
(A) A logo is not clear.
(B) A shipment is late.
(C) A printer is broken.
(D) A name is misspelled.

100. Look at the graphic. What type of business is Universal Solutions?
(A) A hardware company.
(B) A law office.
(C) An auto repair shop.
(D) A marketing agency.

This is the end of the Listening test. Turn to Part 5 in your test book.

GO ON TO THE NEXT PAGE.

READING TEST

In the Reading test, you will read a variety of texts and answer several different types of reading comprehension questions. The entire Reading test will last 75 minutes. There are three parts, and directions are given for each part. You are encouraged to answer as many questions as possible within the time allowed.

You must mark your answers on the separate answer sheet. Do not write your answers in your test book.

PART 5

Directions: A word or phrase is missing in each of the sentences below. Four answer choices are given below each sentence. Select the best answer to complete the sentence. Then mark the letter (A), (B), (C), or (D) on your answer sheet.

101. To access the computer lab, all employees must present their corporate security badge for -------.
(A) inspection
(B) inspecting
(C) inspected
(D inspect

102. The Sunset Bar and Grill will be closed on Saturday, July 26th, ------- a private event.
(A) since
(B) of
(C) along
(D) for

103. While Dr. McGraw is at the conference, please direct all calls to ------- administrative assistant.
(A) he
(B) himself
(C) his
(D) him

104. If you have questions ------- a Suncraft product, please contact our customer service department.
(A) about
(B) against
(C) after
(D) across

105. The Athenian Bookstore on Oak Terrace Boulevard ------- hosts book signings by national authors.
(A) frequented
(B) frequently
(C) frequent
(D) frequency

106. The Tidalwave dishwasher uses ------- filter technology to prevent large particles from clogging your drains.
(A) surprised
(B) pleased
(C) educated
(D) advanced

107. Happy Valley Foods, Inc. ------- its workforce by 10 percent this year.
(A) increase
(B) is increased
(C) will increase
(D) increasing

108. Mr. Thomas wants more ------- about the cost of travel before he can approve the budget.
(A) information
(B) collection
(C) production
(D) reservation

109. Fortunately, Mr. Lathrop was able to rearrange the schedule ------- a problem.
(A) although
(B) except
(C) without
(D) but

110. Over the past decade, Scarsdale Industries ------- the standard for developing innovative industrial ventilation technologies.
(A) has set
(B) will be setting
(C) setting
(D) to set

111. Laurel Canyon can easily be reached ------- taking the Hollywood Hills Rail Line.
(A) by
(B) at
(C) into
(D) to

112. More than 400 employees of Southern Idaho Energy Corp. have ------- completed our engineering skills training course.
(A) successes
(B) successfully
(C) to succeed
(D) succeeded

113. Dalong Bay is a popular tourist location, ------- its mild climate can be enjoyed year-round.
(A) and
(B) how
(C) due to
(D) as if

114. City of Compton employees who have not yet taken vacation days must use ------- by December 31.
(A) their
(B) themselves
(C) they
(D) them

115. Surveys suggest that many Atlas Motors customers choose the Coachman sedan because of its ------- price.
(A) affordably
(B) affording
(C) affordable
(D) afford

116. Our supervisor will decide ------- to purchase the new filing cabinets from Steenburg Office Supply.
(A) so that
(B) even if
(C) whether
(D) neither

117. Five Sister oyster sauce is versatile in its ------- to complement many dishes.
(A) ably
(B) ablest
(C) able
(D) ability

118. Although tickets for the Akron Symphony's summer concert went on sale just yesterday, they have ------- sold out.
(A) never
(B) already
(C) yet
(D) whenever

119. Country Kitchen on Wheels delivers nutritious prepared meals to people who are too ------- to cook for themselves.
(A) busier
(B) busy
(C) busyness
(D) busiest

120. In order to boost morale, Janice Adams, president of Cheer Market, has ------- winter bonuses for all employees.
(A) informed
(B) reached
(C) decided
(D) announced

GO ON TO THE NEXT PAGE

121. For prompt publication of your submission, please ensure that its length and format ------- to the required specifications.
(A) appeal
(B) conform
(C) deliver
(D) attach

122. The relationship between Krause Construction and Boland Engineering, Inc., has been ------- beneficial.
(A) mutually
(B) commonly
(C) dominantly
(D) exactly

123. ------- joining TorpCon, Ms. Gordon served as director of marketing at Boundless.
(A) Prior to
(B) As long as
(C) By the time
(D) Just as

124. -------, instructors at the Institute of Textile Design teach ten courses per week.
(A) Every day
(C) Sooner
(B) Anytime
(D) In many cases

125. Kumar Chiropractic's marketing campaign is ------- new patients.
(A) meant by
(B) attempted to
(C) desired as
(D) intended for

126. ------- our onsite dining facilities, Juan's Bistro can provide full-service catering at businesses or private residences.
(A) For instance
(B) Furthermore
(C) On account of
(D) In addition to

127. Investing in this new software company is probably not a sound idea until we read the ------- of its business plan.
(A) degrees
(B) individuals
(C) resolutions
(D) particulars

128. The committee that was formed ------- workplace diversity at Swift Electronics was highly successful.
(A) to address
(B) was addressing
(C) addressed
(D) has addressed

129. The aim of Motion Consulting is to help inventors ------- their ideas to potential clients.
(A) promote
(B) benefit
(C) invest
(D) create

130. The study on allergies conducted by Saturn Labs yielded results that were ------- to what we expected.
(A) contrary
(B) variable
(C) disobedient
(D) reciprocal

PART 6

Directions: Read the texts that follow. A word or phrase is missing in some of the sentences. Four answer choices are given below each of the sentences. Select the best answer to complete the text. Then mark the letter (A), (B), (C), or (D) on your answer sheet.

Questions 131-134 refer to the following brochure.

Bank of Arizona's services give you the flexibility of paying your bills in a variety of ways. ------- option provides you with the
131.
financial security our customers have come to rely on.

Our online services are designed for maximum ------- of use.
132.

You can budget your monthly expenses by ------- automatic
133.
payments in just a few steps at home and on your mobile phone. -------.
134.

At Bank of Arizona, you're not just a customer—you're a partner!

131. (A) Each
(B) Such
(C) All
(D) One

132. (A) easeful
(B) easily
(C) easy
(D) ease

133. (A) set
(B) to set
(C) seating with
(D) setting up

134. (A) Call us today and learn more about how we can work together to make your banking experience smooth and hassle-free
(B) Leave a message at the tone and a customer service agent will return your call as soon as possible
(C) Enjoy lower interest rates and special discounts on promotional items during the holiday season
(D) Save time and money by opening a direct deposit account with no minimum balance required

GO ON TO THE NEXT PAGE.

November 12

To whom it may concern,

I ------- Ms. Ellen Petsche as a candidate for work in the field of public
   135.

relations. Ms. Petsche ------- at Big Picture PR in New York. Her main
       136.

responsibility here is to promote various events and products for our

company's clientele. Ms. Petsche has worked under my supervision for

the past three years. __-------. I am sure Ms. Petsche will be a great ------- to
    137.   **138.**

any organization that she becomes a part of in the future.

Sincerely,

Iman Aziz

Managing Partner

Big Picture PR

135. (A) regret
(B) recall
(C) relieve
(D) recommend

136. (A) employs
(B) employed
(C) is employed
(D) was employed

137. (A) I particularly value her strong work ethic and excellent communication skills
(B) Let me explain her absence from your most recent visit to our offices
(C) This is the first in a series of promotional tours
(D) Today's event at the convention center has been postponed

138. (A) asset
(B) sign
(C) decision
(D) release

Museum Expansion Plans in Limbo

DALLAS (August 21) —Ron Fogerty, spokesperson for the Dallas Museum of Science and Industry, announced today that the expansion project scheduled to begin next spring has been ------- . **139.** The museum's board of directors had approved a plan to annex the ground floor of the neighboring unoccupied residential tower to create ten additional galleries. ------- , the owner of the adjacent **140.** building has decided not to lease his property to the museum, effectively putting an end to the project. ------- "But **141.** we're not giving up," Mr. Fogerty said, adding that the board will meet next week with architects to discuss the ------- **142.** of adding a fourth floor to the museum.

- *Staff writer*

139. (A) cancelled
(B) renewed
(C) funded
(D) reduced

140. (A) That is
(B) Otherwise
(C) In addition
(D) However

141. (A) The museum has not been expanded since it first opened in 1966.
(B) Donors sipped cocktails and mingled with members of the board.
(C) Renovations are expected to take up to six months.
(D) Scientists from around the world will appear at the grand opening.

142. (A) feasible
(B) feasibility
(C) more feasible
(D) most feasibly

GO ON TO THE NEXT PAGE.

From:	Candace Sikorski <knitter88@qmail.com>
To:	Paolo Minetti <paolo@minettidrapery.com>
Re:	Installation Estimate
Date:	May 15

Dear Ms. Sikorski,

I have taken measurements of the windows in your house where you would like new curtains installed, and I am writing to let you know ___143.___ for the entire project is $773. This includes removing the old curtains, removing the old rods, and installing the new rods and curtains.

Our records show that you have ___144.___ Deep Shale #7781 for the living room and Tropical Blue #8809 for the bedrooms.

We will need two days to complete the labor. Our first available time slot is June 28-29. The ___145.___ available dates are July 2-3. ___146.___.

Best,
Paolo Minetti, Owner
Minetti Drapery, Inc.

143. (A) it will cost
(B) costing that
(C) it is the cost
(D) that the cost

144. (A) selected
(B) delivered
(C) created
(D) solved

145. (A) only
(B) next
(C) recent
(D) upcoming

146. (A) Please remit the past due amount as soon as possible
(B) Please contact me to schedule your appointment
(C) Please keep the windows closed until further notice
(D) Please indicate when you wish to have measurements taken

Directions: In this part you will read a selection of texts, such as magazine and newspaper articles, e-mails, and instant messages. Each text or set of texts is followed by several questions. Select the best answer for each question and mark the letter (A), (B), (C), or (D) on your answer sheet.

Questions 147-148 refer to the following invitation.

It's a girl!
Or at least that's what the doctors say at this point.

You are cordially invited to a baby shower for Julie Chen, Saturday, March 17, from 12:00 to 2:00 P.M.

Tiffany Gardens
234 Highland Road
Kansas City, MO

RSVP by May 1 to Mary Kay Fogerty at 556-3012
Please join us for a non-alcoholic champagne toast to Julie's good fortune!
A light lunch will be served.

147. What is indicated about Julie Chen?
(A) She is pregnant.
(B) She needs help finding a job.
(C) She works from home.
(D) She lives in Kansas City.

148. What is stated about the event?
(A) It will end in the evening.
(B) It will include a meal.
(C) It will feature an open bar.
(D) It will be held on a Friday.

GO ON TO THE NEXT PAGE.

BE THE GUITAR HERO OF YOUR DREAMS!

Howard Gulliver, Professional Guitarist

Do you see yourself on stage playing guitar in front of millions of adoring fans?

Are you a beginning guitarist and want to master the proper skills and techniques of the instrument?

Are you missing that inspirational spark you need to succeed?

Allow me to introduce myself.

Tel: 310-5505

I'm Howard Gulliver and I've been playing guitar professionally for over 25 years. My guitar work has been featured on studio recordings by several major artists including Dark Stars, the Charlie Bing Trio, and Large Marge. I've played in successful bands that have toured the world. With my guidance and the right attitude, you can be on your way to guitar hero status in as little as six weeks. Lessons take place in my home studio, where you can also learn the basics of audio production. My rates are fair and affordable. Call me anytime at 310-5505.

Howard Gulliver 310-5505 | Howard Gulliver 310-5505 | Howard Gulliver 310-5505 | Howard Gulliver 310-5505 | Howard Gulliver 310-5505 | Howard Gulliver 310-5505 | Howard Gulliver 310-5505 | Howard Gulliver 310-5505 | Howard Gulliver 310-5505 | Howard Gulliver 310-5505 | Howard Gulliver 310-5505

149. What is being advertised?
(A) A concert.
(B) A charity event.
(C) Guitar lessons.
(D) A recording studio.

150. What does the writer NOT say about himself?
(A) He has been teaching for 25 years.
(B) He has worked in recording studios.
(C) He has been on tour.
(D) He has played in successful bands.

URGENT MESSAGE

TO: Dr. Benjamin Loeb

FROM : Dr. Michael Font – Good Samaritan Medical Clinic

(Telephone)   Fax   Office Visit

Message:

Please call Iris Montgomery at the San Pedro office at your earliest convenience concerning your application for a summer residency at the clinic. They need to know your specific financial requirements (salary, housing stipend, etc.).

Ms. Montgomery's office number is 815-878-9900

Taken by: Xiao-hua Fang

---

151. What is being requested in the message?
(A) Detailed financial requirements.
(B) Application forms.
(C) Specific dates and locations.
(D) An appointment.

152. Who applied for a residency at the clinic?
(A) Xiao-hua Fang.
(B) Benjamin Loeb.
(C) Michael Font.
(D) Iris Montgomery.

GO ON TO THE NEXT PAGE.

Attention: Rochester Public Transportation Passengers

Because of ongoing construction of the Rochester Metro flood sewer system and associated road repairs on Interstate 90, some light rail services will be temporarily suspended starting on June 15 and continuing through July 15. Passengers are advised that they may need to take alternate routes during this period. All light rail routes will resume their regular schedules on July 16.

Line	Route	Departure	Dates
Green	Downtown to University Boulevard	10-20 mins.	Running as scheduled
Blue	Brighton Street to RSU	30 mins.	Not in Service: June 20 – 25
Red	Keane Armory to Southwest Rochester	Every hour	Not in Service: June 15 – 20
Brown	Union Street Express	5-10 mins.	Running as scheduled
Yellow	Metro Loop	Every hour	Not in Service: July 1 – 15
Orange	East Valley to Irondequoit	Every hour	Not in Service: June 25 – July 1

Refer to the regular schedule for departure and route information.

For additional information or to make an inquiry, visit our Web site at

www.rpt.com.gov or feedback@rpt.com

153. What is the notice about?
    (A) A temporary change in light rail service.
    (B) The removal of some light rail cars.
    (C) A price increase for light rail tickets.
    (D) The addition of new light rail routes.

154. According to the notice, what road is undergoing maintenance?
    (A) Union Street.
    (B) Interstate 90.
    (C) Brighton Street.
    (D) University Boulevard.

155. Which route is scheduled to run most frequently?
    (A) The Blue Line.
    (B) The Red Line.
    (C) The Brown Line.
    (D) The Orange Line.

From:	Crown Financial Consumer Protection <no-reply@crown.com>
To:	Daniel Murray Jr. <danielmurrayjr@britmail.com.uk>
Re:	Fraud Alert
Date:	December 30

Dear Mr. Murray,

Suspicious activity was detected on your Crown credit card account ending in 0033.

The following transaction was recently submitted and flagged for possible fraud.

Vendor name: Data Blitz, Inc.
Transaction code: TT67BX
Amount: $3,357.90
Date of transaction: December 29

If you did not authorize this charge or believe this charge to be an error, please contact our Consumer Fraud Division at (312) 920-0663 as soon as possible. Do not reply to this e-mail. Messages sent to this address will not be answered.

If you no longer wish to receive e-mails concerning unusual transactions, please log in to My Accounts at www.Crown.com.us/accounts.

Thank you for your continued business.
Crown Financial

156. Why was the e-mail sent?
(A) To provide a monthly statement.
(B) To confirm a transaction.
(C) To request updated billing information.
(D) To close an account.

157. What is indicated about Mr. Murray?
(A) His home address has changed.
(B) He is the owner of Costa Mesa Bicycles.
(C) He has a Crown Credit Card.
(D) His credit limit has been reached.

158. How is Mr. Murray instructed to respond?
(A) By making a phone call.
(B) By sending a notarized receipt.
(C) By submitting an application.
(D) By replying to the e-mail.

GO ON TO THE NEXT PAGE

Enjoy the benefits of membership!

When you join the **Parker Sculpture Garden Society**, your dues do more than simply support new exhibits and educational programs for both adults and students of all ages. Basic membership privileges include unlimited free admission to the garden, a 20 percent discount on all purchases in the Sculptor's Studio, exclusive previews of special exhibits, a monthly newsletter, and access to the members-only Sunlight Atrium for special events. To join today, ask for an application form at the information desk, to the left of the front entrance.

159. What is the purpose of this notice?
(A) To describe the sculpture garden.
(B) To sell tickets to an exhibit.
(C) To advertise membership benefits.
(D) To seek donations from the community.

160. Where would this notice most likely appear?
(A) On a local job posting board.
(B) In the gardening section of the newspaper.
(C) In a landscaping magazine.
(D) Near the exit of the Parker Sculpture Garden.

161. According to the notice, what is NOT offered?
(A) Discounts on purchases.
(B) Free publications.
(C) Free art lessons.
(D) Access to a private area.

162. Where is the Parker Sculpture Garden information desk located?
(A) To the right of the entrance.
(B) To the left of the entrance.
(C) In the Sunlight Atrium.
(D) In the Sculptor's Studio.

Questions 163-166 refer to the following article.

Welcome to Sao Paulo, a city on the cusp of resurgence, and an example of prudent urban planning. Not long ago, Sao Paulo residents would have scoffed at the idea of hosting a world-class event like The International Fashion and Design Exposition. Originally held in New York, the exposition has since been held in Milan, Buenos Aires, and Sydney. Now it is Sao Paulo's turn to join the list of distinguished organizers and hosts of the event.

The winning bid to host the exposition caught many Sao Paulo residents off guard, as few expected their city to be chosen in favor of larger, more sophisticated cities with better infrastructure and event facilities. The exposition will be spread across the city, but based in Parque Ibira, the city's greatest urban renewal project. Once home to an industrial area of forgotten factories and a cemetery; Parque Ibira was reclaimed in a span of two years. The three-square-mile area has been revitalized into a modern complex of contemporary pavilions and multi-purpose exhibition halls that will serve as Sao Paulo's thriving commercial center after the event. Come feel the energy.

Sao Paulo - a city with purpose

163. Where was the exposition first held?
    (A) In New York.
    (B) In Buenos Aires.
    (C) In Sydney.
    (D) In Milan.

164. What used to occupy the area that is now Parque Ibira?
    (A) A regional trade center.
    (B) A international airport.
    (C) An industrial district.
    (D) A residential complex.

165. How long did it take to construct the event site?
    (A) 2 years.
    (B) 3 years.
    (C) 5 years.
    (D) 6 years.

166. What is suggested about many Sao Paulo residents?
    (A) They did not expect to win the bid.
    (B) They voted to expand the industrial district.
    (C) They did not support the plan to build a lumber mill.
    (D) They opposed the urban renewal project.

GO ON TO THE NEXT PAGE.

Questions 166-170 refer to the following article.

June 30 - Electria Introduces Another New Whitening Toothpaste

Chicago – Electria, a subsidiary of Smith-Glaxo Inc., has just announced a national product launch for its newest whitening toothpaste, Extra Bright & Shiny. The product will hit the shelves nationwide on July 21, with worldwide distribution expected in early August. ---[1]---.

TV, radio, and social media marketing campaigns will kick off in selected cities (Chicago, New York, and Los Angeles) on July 14. ---[2]---. Print advertisements are scheduled to appear in magazines and newspapers on a regional basis as the launch generates momentum.

This development is the third in a line of new products introduced in the last quarter for the 5-year-old company. ---[3]---.

High Beam, the company's flagship toothpaste and top-seller, suffered a sixteen percent decrease in sales over the last six quarters, prompting Bush Tetra president George Hamilton to initiate an expansion of Electria's product line. ---[4]---. Extra Bright & Shiny was tested in several markets (Orlando, Florida; Detroit, Michigan) where it performed well enough to forecast promising sales.

167. When will the new toothpaste be available nationally?
(A) On June 30.
(B) On July 14.
(C) On July 21.
(D) Sometime in August.

168. Where are social media campaigns NOT scheduled to appear?
(A) In Chicago.
(B) In Orlando.
(C) In Los Angeles.
(D) In New York.

169. What is given as a reason for developing new toothpastes?
(A) Declining sales for current products.
(B) Record-breaking results in test markets.
(C) Firing of a new company president.
(D) Increasing competition from new companies.

170. In which of the positions marked [1], [2], [3] and [4] does the following sentence best belong?

"Other new additions include: Dental Dazzle Blinding White and Sparkle Tooth."
(A) [1]
(B) [2]
(C) [3]
(D) [4]

THE COMPETITIVE EDGE
Greenberg Capital Ventures
November Newsletter

After a distinguished career as a stock analyst with Greenberg Capital Ventures, Sandra Dyke will retire on November 20. Sandra leaves us to spend more time with her family and to pursue her ambitious travel plans. Fortunately, she remains available as an on-call consultant, when she's not on a sailboat headed for the Maldives!

The analytics division will celebrate Dyke's long list of contributions to the company and to the field of bond futures trading at a November 13 reception, to be held from 6:00 p.m. to 10:00 p.m. at the Ponderosa Plaza, Dallas. CEO Skip Gough and executive fund manager Bill Stein will co-host the event.

At Greenberg Capital, Dyke made outstanding strides in the standardization of analytical tools for futures trading. Dyke led her team's implementation of an infinitely more user-friendly bond dividend matrix, which was a godsend to traders. Moreover, Dyke has penned dozens of publications including *The Magic of Stock Analysis*. She is currently working on a software program for GCV scheduled to debut next year. Dyke has also served as the president of Indexes and Futures and as a fellow of the Noonan Freeman Society, and is a lifetime associate of the National Institute of Economics.

Dyke's future research interests include stock analysis software design with a focus on over-the-counter trading.

GCV staff and associates must register before November 1 to attend the reception.

GO ON TO THE NEXT PAGE.

171. What is the main purpose of the article?
    (A) To name an award recipient.
    (B) To report on a speech.
    (C) To introduce a new researcher.
    (D) To announce a retirement.

172. What is NOT listed among Ms. Dyke's future plans?
    (A) Traveling.
    (B) Writing a book.
    (C) Developing a software program.
    (D) Consulting for her colleagues.

173. According to the article, what contributions has Ms. Dyke made to the company?
    (A) She established the analytics division.
    (B) She initiated a partnership with foreign investors.
    (C) She helped design a useful computer software program.
    (D) She led a highly successful sales staff.

174. The word "penned" in paragraph 3, line 4 is the closest in meaning to
    (A) run.
    (B) exposed.
    (C) written.
    (D) distributed.

175. What are prospective attendees asked to do?
    (A) Purchase a stock at market value.
    (B) Register in advance for the event.
    (C) Complete a survey by computer.
    (D) Visit the company's Web site.

From:	Laniah Lewis <laniah@apex.com>
To:	Isaac Brown <brown_direct@carboncopy.com>
Re:	9th Annual Apex Marketing Summit
Date:	March 30

✉ Itinerary.doc 23k

Dear Mr. Brown:

As coordinator of this year's summit, I'm pleased that you have agreed to direct one of our sessions. This year will be my ninth consecutive year organizing the Apex Marketing Summit, and during that time, I have met many people who work at Carbon Copy. In fact, last year, the head of your agency, Ms. Kendra Wilbur was a guest speaker and her presentation on "Big Data: Can vs. Should" inspired many participants.

As you requested when you phoned me last week, your session has been scheduled for the afternoon of April 12. If you check the attached agenda, you will see the title of your presentation listen in the last time slot on that day. If you have any questions, please do not hesitate to contact me at (514) 223-1144.

Thank you very much and I hope you enjoy the experience.

Sincerely,

Laniah Lewis, Apex Summit Coordinator

GO ON TO THE NEXT PAGE

Apex Marketing Summit Agenda
April 10-12
Starworld Plaza Hotel

Thursday, April 10

9:30 A.M.-10:00 A.M.
Opening Ceremony
Starworld Plaza Ballroom

10:15 A.M.-12:00 P.M.
"The Cloud: Risk and Reward"
Coverdale Meeting Room

12:00 Noon-1:15 P.M.
Lunch
Hotel Restaurant

1:30 P.M.-3:00 P.M.
"How to Analyze and Use Your Social Media Data"
Starwood Belle Room

3:15 P.M.-5:00 P.M.
"Paid Media as the New Marketing Model"
Smalley Room

Friday, April 11

9:30 A.M.-10:50 A.M.
"The Model for Successful Content Marketing"
Starworld Plaza Ballroom

11:00 A.M.-12:00 P.M.
"Harnessing Innovation & Creativity"
Starwood Belle Room

12:00 Noon-1:15 P.M.
Lunch
Hotel Restaurant

1:30 P.M.-3:00 P.M.
"The Cutting Edge of Branding"
Colonel Parker Room

3:15 P.M.-5:00 P.M.
"Competitive Advantages"
Executive Meeting Room

Saturday, April 12

9:30 A.M.-10:50 A.M.
"Manage Your Marketing Teams"
Executive Meeting Room

11:00 A.M.-12:00 P.M.
"Effective Marketing Campaigns"
Colonel Parker Room

12:00 Noon-1:15 P.M.
Lunch
Hotel Restaurant

1:30 P.M.-2:30 P.M.
"Building Customer Loyalty"
H. L. Duke Room

2:45 P.M.-3:00 P.M.
Closing Ceremony
Starworld Plaza Ballroom

176. What is the purpose of the e-mail?
(A) To explain the registration process.
(B) To announce a change in the schedule.
(C) To follow up on a phone call.
(D) To offer a position at a conference center.

177. What is true about Laniah Lewis?
(A) She will be introduced to Ms. Wilbur tomorrow.
(B) She cancelled her appointment with Mr. Brown.
(C) She has coordinated a summit before.
(D) She will speak at one of the sessions.

178. When does the conference end?
(A) On Thursday.
(B) On Friday.
(C) On Saturday.
(D) On Sunday.

179. Where does Isaac Brown most likely work?
(A) At an accounting firm.
(B) At an advertising agency.
(C) At a resort hotel.
(D) At a travel agency.

180. Where will Mr. Brown's session happen?
(A) In the Executive Meeting Room.
(B) n the Coverdale Meeting Room.
(C) In the H. L. Duke Room.
(D) In the Starworld Plaza Ballroom.

GO ON TO THE NEXT PAGE.

From:	Joelle Van Stout <jvs@belflex.com>
To:	All staff <A-List.smtp.@belflex.pop.com>
Re:	Annual 10K Run for Charity Event
Date:	June 25

Every year for the past five years, the Belflex Group has participated in the annual Abernathy Foundation 10K fundraising event. Up until now, the event has been held at Riverview Park, but since the park is currently closed for renovations, the run will take place on the former airfield at the Old Point Pleasant Armory. Now in its sixth year, all proceeds for this year's event will be donated to the Greater Cincinnati Literacy Foundation.

The event is scheduled to start at 8:00 a.m. this Saturday, June 30. Please arrive a few minutes early to pick up your running bib number at the entrance to Point Pleasant.

As before, Belflex Group departments will be competing against each other, and the department with the highest score will be treated to an extravagant feast at Giuseppi's Restaurant. If your department wishes to participate in this event, please complete the attached registration form and give it to Lourdes DuPlussaint no later than 4:00 p.m. on June 26, as she needs to confirm our number of participants with Abernathy.

We hope that you will participate in this annual event for a fantastic cause. I look forward to seeing you at Point Pleasant.

Regards,
Joelle Van Stout

From:	Dale Morris <dmorris@Belflex.com>
To:	Joelle Van Stout <jvs@belflex.com>
Re:	Annual 10K Run for Charity Event
Date:	June 26

Dear Lourdes,

Yesterday, I gave you a completed form for the upcoming 10K charity event. The form contains the names of seven individuals here in the compliance department who will be representing this office.

One member, Dan Lorenzo, informed me this morning that he will not be able to participate. Mr. Lorenzo and his wife will be attending a funeral in Cleveland on the very same day as the event. However, an office assistant who started here last week, Ms. Tory Bruge, has volunteered to take Mr. Lorenzo's place. Could you please make this change on the form?

Thank you and we look forward to seeing you this weekend.

Sincerely,
Dale Morris

181. What is the Abernathy Foundation?
  (A) A renowned book publisher.
  (B) A writers' association.
  (C) A local news agency.
  (D) A charity organization.

182. What is mentioned about this year's event?
  (A) It has been postponed for one week.
  (B) It will not be held in the usual location.
  (C) It has fewer participants than last year.
  (D) It will not start until 8:30.

183. What document is Dale Morris referring to in the second e-mail?
  (A) A job evaluation report.
  (B) A billing statement.
  (C) An event registration form.
  (D) A contract renewal slip.

184. Why did Mr. Morris send the e-mail to Ms. DuPlussaint?
  (A) To inquire about starting a company running club.
  (B) To obtain directions to Point Pleasant.
  (C) To request a registration form for an event.
  (D) To inform her of a change in participants.

185. When will Dan Lorenzo attend a funeral?
  (A) June 25.
  (B) June 26.
  (C) June 30.
  (D) June 31.

GO ON TO THE NEXT PAGE.

ProTex Paint Co. is the top paint retailer in West Texas because we make it easy to choose the perfect colors for your home or office.

Browse through hundreds of colors on our Web site, www.protexpaint.com. Select your preferred colors, and we'll send free samples right to your door.

Our color samples are two to three times larger than typical samples found in home-improvement stores and come with self-adhesive backing, so you can easily see how colors will coordinate in your home. When you're ready to begin painting, simply select your chosen colors online, and we'll ship the paint of your choice to arrive at your home within 3-5 business days, or within 2 business days for an additional express shipping fee.

*Actual colors may differ slightly from what appears on your monitor. For this reason, we recommend ordering several samples in similar shades.

#1 Paint Retailer in West Texas

PROTEX PAINT CO.

Tex Industries

www.protexpaint.com

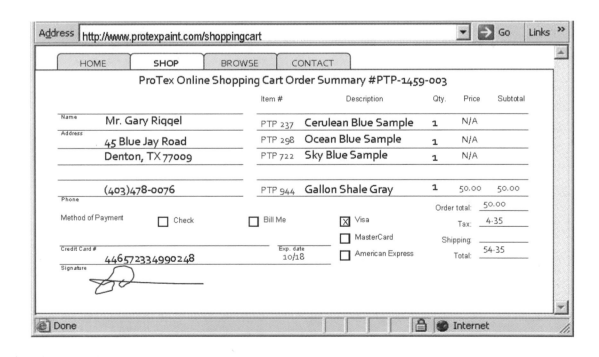

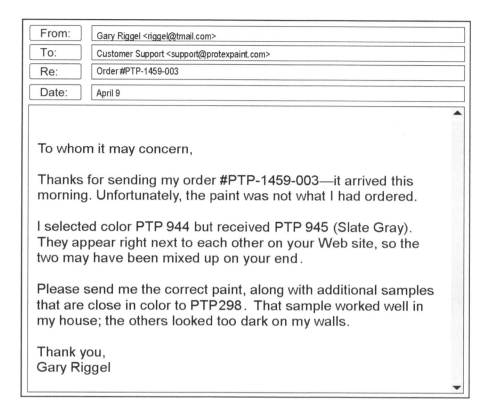

From: Gary Riggel <riggel@tmail.com>

To: Customer Support <support@protexpaint.com>

Re: Order #PTP-1459-003

Date: April 9

To whom it may concern,

Thanks for sending my order #PTP-1459-003—it arrived this morning. Unfortunately, the paint was not what I had ordered.

I selected color PTP 944 but received PTP 945 (Slate Gray). They appear right next to each other on your Web site, so the two may have been mixed up on your end.

Please send me the correct paint, along with additional samples that are close in color to PTP298. That sample worked well in my house; the others looked too dark on my walls.

Thank you,
Gary Riggel

186. In the advertisement, the word "top" in paragraph 1, line 1, is closest in meaning to
(A) important.
(B) upper.
(C) maximum.
(D) favorite.

187. What claim does the advertisement make about ProTex Paint Co.?
(A) They're the top paint retailer in the State of Taxes.
(B) They're the only paint retailer in West Texas.
(C) Their prices are lower.
(D) Their samples are larger.

188. What are ProTex Paint customers advised to do?
(A) Apply an adhesive to color samples.
(B) Visit a store to compare paint colors.
(C) Adjust the color on their computer monitors.
(D) Order samples of several similar colors.

189. What problem did Mr. Riggle mention in his e-mail?
(A) The delivery time was too long.
(B) The instructions were too confusing.
(C) He received the wrong item.
(D) He was charged the wrong price.

190. Which color does Mr. Riggle indicate that he likes?
(A) Cerulean Blue.
(B) Sky Blue.
(C) Ocean Blue.
(D) Slate Gray.

GO ON TO THE NEXT PAGE.

Questions 191-195 refer to the following article, letter, and voucher.

VOLUME 23, ISSUE 7

[MUSIC FACTORY BOISE]

MAY 2017

BRAXTON STAGES COMEBACK

Wyatt Braxton

The idea that Wyatt Braxton is washed up as a country singer due to health-related issues is false.

The 41-year-old, noted for several number one hits including "A Broken Heart is Still Broken" three years ago, and last year's "The Loneliest Wolf", gives an excellent performance in his new release, "The Birth of Calamity".

Based on the true story of Serj "Marshall" Branislav, the haunting folk tune tells the story of the struggles of a small group of Serbian settlers in southern Idaho.

Braxton's voice, with help from songwriter Phil Blott, takes you on an emotional journey as Branislav strives to build Idaho's very first Serbian town, Calamity. This song is an excellent tribute to the 150th anniversary of the founding of Calamity.

The song's producer, Lou Lange, believes that nobody could have given a better performance than Wyatt Braxton. Lange has produced over 45 Top 10 hits during his career, including the song that launched Braxton to stardom 20 years ago titled "My Lover's Lover."

"The Birth of Calamity" will be available for download from yTunes on May 12, coinciding with the launch of Braxton's first U.S. tour in five years. Braxton's tour will open at Music Factory Boise.

UPCOMING SHOWS AT THE FACTORY

- May 12—Wyatt Braxton
- May 13—Dirty Dave and the Sheep
- May 16—GETGO
- May 18-20—Ben Benson's Jazz Combo
- May 25—Fast Cats, Bed Song, Vipers
- May 27—Punk Explosion

Music Factory Boise

416 S. 9th Street

Boise, ID 83702

Tel: (604) 581-4344   Fax: (604) 581-4341

May 5

Sonya Freshmore

235 Franklin Road

Hidden Springs, ID 83701

Dear Ms. Freshmore,

During one of many events at Music Factory Boise approximately two weeks ago, you entered a contest for the chance to win a pair of tickets to see Wyatt Braxton perform at our venue on May 12. Congratulations! Your name was drawn from over 3,000 entries! The ticket voucher attached to this letter may be redeemed at the box office on the day of the performance. Please read the terms and conditions before redeeming. Thanks for supporting Music Factory Boise and enjoy the show!

Sincerely,

Daxx Dennis, Director of Operations

Music Factory Boise

GO ON TO THE NEXT PAGE.

MUSIC FACTORY BOISE

TICKET VOUCHER

TERMS AND CONDITIONS

GOOD FOR TWO TICKETS

Performance: Wyatt Braxton

Date: May 12

You may only exchange this voucher for tickets to the performance at the time of redemption. This voucher may not be exchanged for tickets already supplied, other goods or cash, and are not transferable for value.

The bearer of the voucher must present a government ID (driver's license, student ID, etc.) This voucher cannot be replaced if lost or stolen.

Music Factory Boise reserves the right, at its sole discretion, to change, modify, add, or remove portions of these Terms and Conditions of Sale at any time.

---

191. According to the review, why was Wyatt Braxton's career thought to be over?
(A) Health-related problems.
(B) Poor sales performances.
(C) A highly-publicized drug scandal.
(D) Lack of record label support.

192. Why was "The Birth of Calamity" written?
(A) To raise money for a charity organization.
(B) To document the life of Natasha Davis.
(C) To celebrate the establishment of a town.
(D) To generate publicity for an online game.

193. What did Sonya Freshmore do at the Music Factory Boise?
(A) She performed some of her new material.
(B) She entered a contest.
(C) She met Lou Lange.
(D) She received an award.

194. In the letter, the word "drawn" in paragraph 2, line 3, is closest in meaning to
(A) exhausted.
(B) selected.
(C) repeated.
(D) interpreted.

195. What does Sonya Freshmore need to do in order to claim the voucher?
(A) Send an email to the venue.
(B) Present a valid ID at the box office.
(C) Show proof of purchase to the cashier.
(D) Exchange the tickets for cash value.

Street Rider Magazine

VOLUME 3, ISSUE 9   JUNE

The Rolls Royce of Helmets

THE ROLLS ROYCE of motorcycle helmets, the new Groessler C3 Pro has been designed to improve on the original C3, which was already one of the quietest and most technologically advanced helmets to date.

Designed by company founder Nick Groessler, the C3 Pro will be available in stores all over North America starting mid-August.

According to Mr. Groessler, his interest in helmet design began when he was an apprentice at Fenske Motor Werks in Munich, Germany. To pay for his living expenses, Groessler obtained a part-time job as a service technician at Crusher, the largest motorsports super store in Europe. Following his apprenticeship, Schberth returned to his hometown of Orlando, Florida, where he worked for two years as an assistant manager at a small skateboard shop named Freewheel. However, Groessler was more interested in motorcycles than skateboards, so he moved to Chicago last year and opened his own design shop in Wicker Park, Groessler Industrial Safety, Co.

Groessler is pleased with the success of his helmets and other accessories, but noted that since he is only in his late-20s, he plans to expand his business into other areas, including his own line of high-end motorcycles.

- Adrian Swift

Groessler C3

GO ON TO THE NEXT PAGE.

From:	Mark Lindsay <hotrod44@unmail.com>
To:	Nick Groessler< nick@groessler.com>
Re:	Congratulations!
Date:	June 29

Hey Nick,

While eating breakfast yesterday morning, I came across an article about your helmets and I wanted to congratulate you. I have already found many stores here in Orlando that carry items of your brand. It is fantastic that you have turned your dream into a reality. You always talked about it when we worked together at Crusher, and it's a reality!

By the way, I will be in Chicago during the second weekend of August and I thought I could take you out to dinner to celebrate. I'll be staying with my cousin, Jerry Pratt, who lives at Milwaukee and Damen Ave., which is just a block east of your shop. I'll be sure to drop by.

Again, congratulations and I'm looking forward to seeing you again.

Mark

196. What does the article mainly discuss?
(A) The closure of a local factory.
(B) The grand opening of a company.
(C) The rising cost of motorcycles in Germany.
(D) The upcoming release of a product.

197. What is true about Nick Groessler?
(A) He is from Munich.
(B) He is 35 years old.
(C) He attended college in Orlando.
(D) He runs his own business.

198. Why did Mark Lindsey send the e-mail to Nick Groessler?
(A) To provide his cousin's address.
(B) To arrange a photo shoot for an ad.
(C) To obtain details of an advertising campaign.
(D) To extend congratulations.

199. What is indicated about Mr. Groessler's shop?
(A) It has not been very successful.
(B) It was founded a decade ago.
(C) It is near Jerry Pratt's home.
(D) It will soon relocate to another city.

200. Where did Mr. Groessler and Mr. Lindsey work together?
(A) In Orlando.
(B) In Chicago.
(C) In Milwaukee.
(D) In Munich.

Stop! This is the end of the test. If you finish before time is called, you may go back to Parts 5, 6, and 7 and check your work.

New TOEIC Listening Script

PART 1

1. (   ) (A) The man is a plumber.
   (B) The man is an architect.
   (C) The man is a chef.
   (D) The man is a bus driver.

2. (   ) (A) Some people are relaxing at the beach.
   (B) Some people are playing music on the sidewalk.
   (C) Some people are setting up a tent in a field.
   (D) Some people are preparing food in a kitchen.

3. (   ) (A) The woman is trying on a dress.
   (B) The woman is carrying a suitcase.
   (C) The woman is wearing house slippers.
   (D) The woman is looking at her phone.

4. (   ) (A) This is an office.
   (B) This is a warehouse.
   (C) This is a bank vault.
   (D) This is a cafeteria.

5. (   ) (A) The girl is using a paintbrush.
   (B) The girl is using a calculator.
   (C) The girl is using a typewriter.
   (D) The girl is using a curling iron.

6. (   ) (A) The boy is riding a bicycle.
   (B) The boy is riding a skateboard.
   (C) The boy is riding a pony.
   (D) The boy is riding a roller coaster.

GO ON TO THE NEXT PAGE

PART 2

7. (   ) Where did you get these party invitations printed?
    (A) I'll be back on Saturday.
    (B) Before the event.
    (C) At a local copy shop.

8. (   ) When will the recreation center open?
    (A) To renovate the gymnasium.
    (B) On April 15.
    (C) It's on Laguna Boulevard.

9. (   ) Which preschool did you choose for your daughter?
    (A) The rest of our family.
    (B) The service was excellent.
    (C) Happy Kids Academy.

10. (   ) Who will be installing the security cameras in the warehouse?
    (A) Shannon O'Brien will.
    (B) On Monday.
    (C) It's for our protection.

11. (   ) Where will the jazz concert be held?
    (A) At the Civic Auditorium.
    (B) She used to be a drummer.
    (C) No, tickets are still available.

12. (   ) How should I ship the order to the customer in Seattle?
    (A) No, I forgot to bring it.
    (B) Please use the overnight delivery service.
    (C) It's in the box.

13. (   ) This sweater is too tight on me, isn't it?
    (A) It's quite warm today.
    (B) Yes, it's a little snug.
    (C) For here or to go?

14. (   ) Why did you switch cell phone carriers?
    (A) Because I got a better deal.
    (B) Call me in the morning.
    (C) At the electronics store.

15. (   ) Where is the information desk for the art museum?
 (A) The painting isn't for sale.
 (B) It's just inside the main entrance.
 (C) The museum curator.

16. (   ) Who's the new director of the compliance division?
 (A) It's sometime in July.
 (B) They must be in the warehouse.
 (C) Kim Phelps is now in charge.

17. (   ) Didn't George fax you the missing invoices?
 (A) The price hasn't changed.
 (B) Yes, I received them this morning.
 (C) There's one leaving at 6.

18. (   ) Why has the budget been cut this year?
 (A) Back in July.
 (B) The company is losing money.
 (C) Yes, that's the idea.

19. (   ) I heard that the community center is closed for renovations.
 (A) I can help you fix it.
 (B) Every day on my way home from work.
 (C) Yes, until next month.

20. (   ) Would you like to try the shirt in a smaller size?
 (A) No, this one fits perfectly.
 (B) Here's your receipt.
 (C) Behind the counter.

21. (   ) Do you know when the inventory reports are due?
 (A) Approximately $5,000.
 (B) He sold it on a Web site.
 (C) Tuesday next week.

22. (   ) Management will announce a plan to upgrade our Internet servers.
 (A) That's a good deal.
 (B) When is that supposed to happen?
 (C) We're going there after lunch.

GO ON TO THE NEXT PAGE.

23. (　　) You're in the market for a studio apartment, aren't you?
   (A) How about 3 o'clock on Friday?
   (B) Actually, I'd prefer a 1-bedroom.
   (C) It overlooks the waterfront.

24. (　　) Is the annual shareholders meeting in Los Angeles or New York this year?
   (A) It starts on April 1st.
   (B) General operating expenses.
   (C) They decided on Boston instead.

25. (　　) Could you put these returned items back on the shelves, please?
   (A) Try the billing department.
   (B) Where does this one belong?
   (C) Here's a purchase order.

26. (　　) What's in that cabinet in the break room?
   (A) That's where we keep our office supplies.
   (B) Or you could stack them on his desk.
   (C) Yes, back to the laboratory.

27. (　　) Don't you and Don Stevens belong to the same country club?
   (A) Generally an hour or two.
   (B) Yes, I run into him there from time to time.
   (C) The event coordinator.

28. (　　) Was the new receptionist trained to use the intercom system?
   (A) The bus doesn't stop at this station.
   (B) The seminar starts at 2:00.
   (C) I'm pretty sure she was.

29. (　　) If you'd like to check out the apartment tomorrow, I'll be there all afternoon.
   (A) I could probably drop by around 4.
   (B) All of the employees.
   (C) No, I haven't seen it.

30. (　　) There's only one customer lingering in the dining room.
   (A) I'll let the manager know.
   (B) The house next door.
   (C) No! I may need to have my eyes examined.

31. (   ) Do you know who will replace Bryan when he transfers to the Cleveland branch?
  (A) On April 15th, I reckon.
  (B) Leslie delivered the lunch order.
  (C) Not yet. We're still interviewing candidates.

PART 3

Questions 32 through 34 *refer to the following conversation.*

W : I bought this watch from your shop last month. And yesterday, the clasp on the wristband fell off. Can you fix it here?

M : I'm sorry but the person who does the repairs is at lunch right now. If you leave the watch here, I'll make sure he fixes it as soon as he returns.

W : OK, I have some errands to run, so I will stop back later in the afternoon.

32. (   ) What is the woman asking about?
  (A) A refund.
  (B) A job.
  (C) A repair.
  (D) A sale.

33. (   ) Why does the man apologize?
  (A) An item is out of stock.
  (B) An employee is not available.
  (C) A store policy has changed.
  (D) A fee is charged for a service.

34. (   ) What does the woman say she will do in the afternoon?
  (A) Return to the shop.
  (B) Submit an application.
  (C) Confirm a payment.
  (D) Call a vendor.

Questions 35 through 37 *refer to the following conversation.*

M : Hi, my name's Lou Ferragamo. I ordered some advertising stickers for my business and they're supposed to be ready today.

W : Sure. Let me bring up the order in our computer system. Hmm... Ferragamo? I don't see anything here.

GO ON TO THE NEXT PAGE.

M : It may be listed under Paramount Landscaping. I stopped in and paid for them the other day.

W : Oh, there it is. We had the order registered under your company name. Yes, the stickers are ready, but do you have a copy of the invoice with you? Our computer system doesn't show that the order has been paid for.

M : //That's going to be a problem. //However, I did pay with my credit card.

W : I see. Sometimes there's a delay in processing credit card payments. Do you have the card with you? I can run a cross-check to see if it's in our system, but simply hasn't posted yet.

35. (　　) Why did the man come to the print shop?
    (A) To inquire about a discount.
    (B) To pick up an order.
    (C) To complain about a service.
    (D) To request express delivery.

36. (　　) What does the woman say about the account?
    (A) It is registered under the company name.
    (B) It has not been activated.
    (C) It is missing an address.
    (D) It is eligible for an upgrade.

37. (　　) Why does the man say, "That's going to be a problem"?
    (A) He lost his credit card.
    (B) He doesn't have the invoice.
    (C) He forgot his ID.
    (D) He doesn't like the sticker design.

Questions 38 through 40 refer to the following conversation.

M : Next customer, please. This register is open if you're ready to make your purchases.

W : Thanks. I'm going to buy this vacuum cleaner, but first I'd like to speak to a manager about the salesperson who just spent half an hour helping me, Rusty Evans. He was knowledgeable and patient as he carefully explained the features of all the different vacuum models.

M : That sounds like Rusty. He has a lot of experience with household appliances. If you'd like, rather than speaking to our manager, you can visit our website and fill out a questionnaire about your shopping experience today.

W : I could do that, but I'm here now, and I'd really like to speak personally with a manager.

M : OK. Just one moment. I'll call upstairs and see if she's available.

38. (   ) Where are the speakers most likely to be?
    (A) At a car dealership.
    (B) At a utility company office.
    (C) At an appliance store.
    (D) At a garden center.

39. (   ) What does the woman want to talk to a manager about?
    (A) Long waiting times.
    (B) A misleading advertisement.
    (C) A helpful employee.
    (D) High-quality merchandise.

40. (   ) What will the man do next?
    (A) Return at another time.
    (B) Visit a website.
    (C) Contact his manager.
    (D) Read a manual.

Questions 41 through 43 refer to the following conversation with three speakers.

Woman A : It's good to see you, Mr. and Mrs. Lambert. Before we start going over your restaurant's finances for this quarter, you mentioned over the phone that you were thinking about expanding your business.

M : Yes, the electronics shop next door is closing. So, we'd like to rent that space. That way, we would double the size of our dining area.

Woman B : And so we wanted to ask you what financial considerations we should factor in.

Woman A : Well, increasing your restaurant's seating capacity doesn't always mean more profit. You might be bringing in more business, but in that case you'd probably need to hire another cook to help keep up with the orders.

Woman B : Plus, we'll be paying more in rent.

M : Right. So, would it be possible for you to create a cost analysis report so that we can get a better sense of whether or not this idea would be profitable?

41. (   ) Who, most likely, is Woman A?
    (A) A restaurant cook.
    (B) An architect.
    (C) A financial adviser.
    (D) A flower shop owner.

GO ON TO THE NEXT PAGE

42. (　　) What are the Lamberts considering doing?
    (A) Leasing out their apartment.
    (B) Expanding their business.
    (C) Opening a bank account.
    (D) Changing his profession.

43. (　　) What does the man ask Woman B to do?
    (A) Prepare a report.
    (B) Order some equipment.
    (C) Create a design.
    (D) Sign a contract.

Questions 44 through 46 _refer to the following conversation._

W : Excuse me, I visited this museum a couple of months ago. And I remember that you had an exhibit of Native American Indian artifacts. I thought it was in the south wing but I can't find it. Could you tell me if the exhibit's still here?

M : Yes, it is. But we recently moved it down stairs. It's in the gallery across from the museum cafeteria. Here, I'll show you on the map.

W : Oh, great. Do you also have a brochure about the exhibit?

M : Yes, and in case you're interested, there's a video on the history of the Cherokee Nation starting in the theater in 10 minutes. If you hurry, you can still make it in time.

44. (　　) Where does the conversation most likely take place?
    (A) At a concert hall.
    (B) At a photography studio.
    (C) At a toy store.
    (D) At a museum.

45. (　　) According to the man, what has recently changed?
    (A) An entrance fee has increased.
    (B) Memberships are now available.
    (C) An exhibit has been relocated.
    (D) A building addition has been completed.

46. (　　) Why does the man encourage the woman to hurry?
    (A) An event is expected to be crowded.
    (B) A video is about to begin.
    (C) A building is closing soon.
    (D) Supplies are limited.

Man A : Hello, Ms. Rogers and Mr. Fielding. Thanks again to both of you for agreeing to participate in today's seminar. As two of our city's most successful real estate agents, could you explain what you think makes you so successful? Ms. Rogers, I'll ask you first.

W : I really think it's my knowledge of the area. Since I grew up in Chicago, I have a good understanding of our neighborhoods and particularly the housing market.

Man A : Mr. Fielding?

Man B : I agree with Ms. Rogers. Knowing the market is essential. However, for me, developing relationships with my clients has been the key to my success. Especially when I was just getting started in the industry and I didn't have a lot of local contacts. Every single relationship was one more step toward success.

W : That's very true, Mr. Fielding.

Man A : Speaking of agents just getting started in the business, what advice would you give to newbies?

Man B : Exactly what I just said. Build solid relationships, one by one, and put in the effort to maintain those relationships.

47. (   ) Where are the speakers?
      (A) At a sales conference.
      (B) At a real estate seminar.
      (C) At an open auction.
      (D) At a graduation ceremony.

48. (   ) What does the woman say makes her successful?
      (A) Her ability to handle multiple projects.
      (B) Her organizational skills.
      (C) Her international experience.
      (D) Her knowledge of the area.

49. (   ) What advice does Man B/Mr. Fielding give?
      (A) Set personal goals at the start of projects.
      (B) Build relationships with clients.
      (C) Stay up to date on industry trends.
      (D) Collaborate with other departments.

GO ON TO THE NEXT PAGE.

W : Hi. There was a note in my mailbox saying that a package was left here at the front desk for me. My name is Glover. G-L-O-V-E-R.

M : Hmm. Do you live in this apartment building? I don't see your name on the list of residents in my computer records.

W : Oh, I just moved in on Monday so that's probably why I'm not in your records. I'm in apartment 307-C.

M : OK, but could you please show me a copy of your lease agreement? I just need some kind of verification before I can give you the package.

W : Um, I don't have my lease on me, but I have a driver's license, and obviously, I have a key to enter the building and open my mailbox.

M : Fine. Please, let me see your ID.

50. (   ) What does the woman want to do?
     (A) Make a payment.
     (B) Claim a package.
     (C) Check in to a hotel.
     (D) Visit a friend.

51. (   ) What is the most likely reason that the woman's name is missing from the list?
     (A) She is a new resident.
     (B) She is a former employee.
     (C) Her subscription was not renewed.
     (D) Her name was misspelled.

52. (   ) What does the man initially ask for?
     (A) An identification card.
     (B) A contract.
     (C) An e-mail address.
     (D) A contact name.

Questions 53 through 55 _refer to the following conversation._

W : Good Morning. I wonder if the library carries a book I'm looking for. It's called One True Vision. The author is Sarah Fleet.

M : Umm, I know we have the book, but our database shows that all our copies are out on loan right now. The Brookline Library has one and we have an interlibrary borrowing program with them. If you'd like, I can have the book sent here for you to borrow.

W : Oh great. Is there a charge for this service?

M : Yes there is. It's a dollar and it will take two to three days for the book to get here.

53. (   ) Who is the man most likely to be?
      (A) An author.
      (B) An accountant.
      (C) A librarian.
      (D) A bank clerk.

54. (   ) What does the man offer to do?
      (A) Sign a form.
      (B) Obtain a book.
      (C) Create an account.
      (D) Copy a document.

55. (   ) Why will the woman be charged a fee?
      (A) For canceling a reservation.
      (B) For renewing a membership.
      (C) For using a special service.
      (D) For replacing a lost card.

Questions 56 through 58 *refer to the following conversation and list.*

W : Um... I just found out I'll be doing some international travel later this year. So I'd like to apply for a passport.

M : Are you applying for your first passport?

W : Yes, I am.

M : OK, here's a brief list of the required documents and a form. When you have them all in order, then you can submit an application.

W : Right. I guess it normally takes four to six weeks to receive the passport, but is there any way I can get it sooner?

M : Yes, there's an option called expedited service. It's an additional 60 dollars and you'll get your passport in seven business days.

56. (   ) What does the woman want to do?
      (A) Make an airline reservation.
      (B) Renew a driver's license.
      (C) Apply for a research grant.
      (D) Obtain a passport.

GO ON TO THE NEXT PAGE

57. (　　) What does the woman inquire about?

    (A) Citizenship.

    (B) Airfares.

    (C) Expedited service.

    (D) Travel times.

58. (　　) Look at the graphic. Which of the following is NOT required for a first-time passport?

    (A) An original birth certificate.

    (B) Proof of identity.

    (C) Four photographs.

    (D) A 60 dollar fee.

FIRST-TIME PASSPORT REQUIREMENTS

● **Original Birth Certificate**

● **Proof of Identity (Driver's License or State-issued ID <u>only</u>)**

● **4 – 2"x2" photographs**

● **Completed Form DS-2310**

Questions 59 through 61 _refer to the following conversation and list._

M : Thanks for inviting me for an interview here at Universal Media, Ms. Feinstein. I'm really hoping to work for a major media company like yours.

W : I'm glad you could make it, Adam. Your academic advisor, Oliver Brown, used to work with us here and he spoke very highly of you. He says you have tremendous potential.

M : Oh, well thank you. I'm really hoping to start making use of my degree in mass communications.

W : When I looked at your resume, I was quite impressed. Now, we don't currently have any full-time job openings for recent graduates. However, I wanted to discuss the possibility of your joining us for an internship. It could be a good opportunity for you to gain practical experience on a variety of media projects.

59. (　　) Where does the woman work?

    (A) At a university.

    (B) At a television station.

    (C) At a public library.

    (D) At a media company.

60. (   ) How does the woman know Oliver Brown?
   (A) He recently submitted a resume.
   (B) He is a local celebrity.
   (C) They are making a film together.
   (D) They used to work at the same company.

61. (   ) Look at the graphic. Which internship would the man most likely be interested in?
   (A) Accounting and Finance.
   (B) Public Relations.
   (C) Art and Design.
   (D) Staging and Lighting.

Internships Available at Universal Media

Accounting and Finance
Public Relations
Art and Design
Staging and Lighting
Post-Production

Questions 62 through 64 refer to the following conversation and directory.

M : Hello, I'm staying in room 1231 and I was woken up this morning by what sounded like jackhammers. I've had a long week of business travel and was really hoping to be able to sleep as late as possible.

W : I'm very sorry, sir. There's a construction crew working on the building next to our hotel. We've already spoken to them out about starting later in the morning.

M : Well, just in case they don't start later, is there a place nearby where I can get some earplugs?

W : As a matter of fact, we carry them in the gift shop.

62. (   ) Where does the woman most likely work?
   (A) At a movie theater.
   (B) At a restaurant.
   (C) At a hotel.
   (D) At an architectural firm.

GO ON TO THE NEXT PAGE.

63. (   ) What is causing a problem?

     (A) Noise from construction work.

     (B) A shortage of trained staff.

     (C) A delayed opening.

     (D) An incorrect bill.

64. (   ) Look at the graphic. What number will the man probably call?

     (A) 110.

     (B) 112.

     (C) 114.

     (D) 116.

SERVICE DIRECTORY	
Front Desk	0
Housekeeping	110
Room Service	112
Concierge	114
Gift Shop	116

Questions 65 through 67 refer to the following conversation.

M : Hi, I'm the director of the Jet Stream Orchestra. Next May we'll be traveling overseas to perform a series of concerts on our first European tour. And you come highly recommended for the tours you've arranged for other orchestras.

W : I'd be glad to help. I've been working in the tourism industry for almost a decade, and before that, I was a professional cello player myself so I understand your needs.

M : That's great. I'm a bit concerned about traveling by air with the instruments. They are very delicate and valuable. Is there a way to make sure they won't be damaged?

W : Most of the instruments are OK as carry-on baggage inside the plane cabin so the musicians can keep an eye on them, but the bigger instruments obviously take up more space, so extra tickets will need to be purchased. It's expensive, but it's the safest way to transport instruments.

65. (   ) Who is the woman most likely to be?

     (A) A hotel manager.

     (B) A tour operator.

     (C) A music instructor.

     (D) A flight attendant.

66. (　　) What is the man concerned about?
  - (A) The size of some rooms.
  - (B) An extra storage fee.
  - (C) Some travel connections.
  - (D) The safe transport of instruments.

67. (　　) What does the woman suggest?
  - (A) Purchasing additional tickets.
  - (B) Talking to a security guard.
  - (C) Contacting the vendor directly.
  - (D) Making a detailed schedule.

Questions 68 through 70 *refer to the following conversation and schedule.*

W : Hi, Kevin. I noticed you weren't at this morning's meeting. Is everything OK?

M : Oh, yeah, Lydia. I'm fine. I was just late because of traffic. I've never seen such congestion downtown. It took me almost an hour to get through the Madison Tunnel.

W : Now that I bike to work, I usually take the side streets where there's less traffic. And I bet it would save you a lot of time if you avoided the tunnel all together.

M : You know, Tom said he's changing our schedule starting next week. I asked to be on the closing shift, so I should be avoiding most of the heavy traffic from now on.

68. (　　) Look at the graphic. According to the new schedule, what time will the man get off work?
  - (A) 5:30 p.m.
  - (B) 7:00 p.m.
  - (C) 8:30 p.m.
  - (D) 10:00 p.m.

NEW SCHEDULE BEGINNING WEEK OF AUGUST 3	
Tom K. (manager)	7:30 a.m. – 5:30 p.m.
Pete L.	9:00 a.m. – 7:00 p.m.
Lydia O.	10:30 a.m. – 8:30 p.m.
Kevin J.	12:00 p.m. – 10:00 p.m.

GO ON TO THE NEXT PAGE.

69. (   ) What does the woman recommend?
    (A) Taking a different route.
    (B) Reviewing some documents.
    (C) Biking to work.
    (D) Making copies.

70. (   ) Why did the man miss the meeting?
    (A) He had another appointment.
    (B) He woke up late.
    (C) He was caught in traffic.
    (D) He was preparing a presentation.

PART 4

Questions 71 through 73 refer to the following excerpt from a meeting.

Does everyone have a copy of the report? OK, good. So I called this meeting to discuss our contract with Indus Outsourcing and to decide whether they should continue to handle our customer service call center. I… uh… had a discussion with their people yesterday, and I'm a little troubled by their attitude. They seem much more focused on cutting their costs than they are on providing customer service. //Here's the deal. //If we decide to end this business relationship, we'll need to pay them for the balance of their one-year contract. Please take a minute to look at the figures on the balance sheet of the report. You'll see we owe them quite a bit. Is it going to be worth cutting our losses at this point?

71. (   ) What bothers the woman about Indus Outsourcing?
    (A) Their request to revise a contract.
    (B) Their focus on cost cutting.
    (C) Their failure to meet deadlines.
    (D) Their problems with staffing.

72. (   ) What does the woman mean when she says, "Here's the deal"?
    (A) She has found what she was looking for.
    (B) She will introduce a point to consider.
    (C) She will demonstrate a product.
    (D) She has forgotten a word.

73. (   ) What are the listeners asked to look at?
  (A) A list of agencies.
  (B) A business report.
  (C) An advertisement.
  (D) A travel itinerary.

Questions 74 through 76 _refer to the following announcement._

Good afternoon and welcome aboard Geneva Air flight number 3L6. My name is Anthony and I'm your senior flight attendant today. Along with my associates, Kim, Jill, and Ronaldo, I promise to take good care of you today. I've been asked to make the following announcement by Geneva Air ground personnel at departure Gate 15. A white Samsung Galaxy smartphone was found on a chair in the departure area of Gate 15 soon after the flight was called for boarding. Please check to make sure you're not missing your phone and push the call button above your seat if you believe it belongs to you. As our team prepares the plane for an on-time departure, a video describing the safety features of this aircraft will be shown on the overhead monitors. Thank you for your attention and your cooperation.

74. (   ) Where does the announcement take place?
  (A) In a café.
  (B) In a hardware store.
  (C) On a ferryboat.
  (D) On an airplane.

75. (   ) What is the main topic of this announcement?
  (A) A change in a schedule.
  (B) Weekly specials.
  (C) An item that has just been found.
  (D) A service that was recently introduced.

76. (   ) What will most likely happen next?
  (A) A policy will be updated.
  (B) A video will be shown.
  (C) A group will be seated.
  (D) A price will be reduced.

GO ON TO THE NEXT PAGE.

Hello, everyone, and welcome to the training session on using the new facilities management software. Today we're going to practice using basic features you need to be familiar with when you work at the front desk. We'll go over how to check room availability, generate and adjust invoices for the guests, and process payments. I think this new software will save you a lot of time when performing your front desk duties. I know we have problems with our current software being really slow. This application truly is much better.

77. (   ) Who are the listeners most likely to be?
(A) Game developers.
(B) Mail clerks.
(C) Hotel staff.
(D) Restaurant managers.

78. (   ) What will the listeners do at the workshop?
(A) Learn to use new software.
(B) Develop goals for the upcoming year.
(C) Discuss customer feedback.
(D) Participate in role-playing activities.

79. (   ) What does the speaker expect will happen?
(A) There will be fewer billing errors.
(B) Employees will work more efficiently.
(C) Customers will write positive reviews.
(D) Sales will increase.

Hurry in to Fashion Emporium this week to take advantage of our huge summer sale. Men's and women's summer styles are now half price. Receive 50% off all in-store purchases. This week only, you can save on the latest fashions whether you're preparing for a business meeting or a trip to the beach. To receive inside information about our newest offers, please sign up to be added to our mailing list at www.fashionemporium.com.

80. (　　) What type of business is being advertised?
  (A) A clothing shop.
  (B) A hair salon.
  (C) A travel agency.
  (D) A computer store.

81. (　　) According to the speaker, what will be available this week?
  (A) A free class.
  (B) Longer hours.
  (C) A new location.
  (D) A 50 percent discount.

82. (　　) Why does the speaker suggest listeners visit their Web site?
  (A) To sign up for the mailing list.
  (B) To read customer reviews.
  (C) To request technical help.
  (D) To make an appointment.

Questions 83 through 85 _refer to the following advertisement and website._

Have you recently been in an auto accident? Did you have insurance? Are you currently driving with a suspended license? If you are, you need talk to an experienced attorney here at Jasper & Jasper Law. We provide quality legal services for anyone who needs legal representation in traffic court. And unlike our competitors, we offer 24-hour online consultation. We're here when YOU need us, and we'll tell you how quickly and cheaply your case can be resolved. Want to avoid a possible jail sentence or lengthy community service? Contact one of our online consultants at www.jandjlaw.com/ and find out how we can make it happen for you!

83. (　　) What is being advertised?
  (A) A publishing company.
  (B) A job placement agency.
  (C) A law firm.
  (D) A business school.

GO ON TO THE NEXT PAGE

84. (   ) What advantage does the speaker mention?
    (A) An online consultation.
    (B) A driving certificate.
    (C) Discounted membership.
    (D) Free legal advice.

85. (   ) Please look at the graphic. What is required to access an online consultant?
    (A) A current driver's license.
    (B) An email address.
    (C) A verification code.
    (D) A cell phone number.

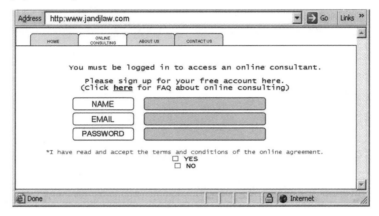

Questions 86 through 88 _refer to an excerpt from a meeting._

Thanks for making time for this meeting, everyone. I wanted to bring the entire staff together to talk about a major change to the music festival we're organizing for next year. The board of directors has reviewed our current list of performers, and they feel that there should be more variety. So instead of just focusing on artists from North America, they want us to include an international stage. //This is not up to me. //It's coming straight from the board. So… Over the course of this week, we need to put together lists of potential foreign artists that we can feature at the festival. Let's take some time right now to start brainstorming and see what we can come up with as a group.

86. (   ) Why are the people meeting?
    (A) To discuss a festival change.
    (B) To watch a selection of films.
    (C) To greet some international visitors.
    (D) To vote for a new board member.

87. (　　) What needs to be added to the schedule?
    (A) A keynote speaker.
    (B) A banquet location.
    (C) Another music category.
    (D) Actors' interviews.

88. (　　) Why does the man say, "This is not up to me"?
    (A) He took part in the discussion.
    (B) He prefers international music.
    (C) He suggested they include more variety.
    (D) He may not agree with the idea.

Questions 89 through 91 _refer to the following telephone message and email attachment._

Hello, Steve. This is Janet Rossi from the human resources department. I'm calling all the project managers to let everyone know that the budgeting seminar, originally scheduled for today, is being postponed until tomorrow. Sorry for the late notice. Although the time's been changed to 1:30 tomorrow afternoon, the meeting will still be held in conference room 2A. I'll send out the meeting agenda by email to everyone in the next hour or so. But be sure to read it so you know how the session relates to the projects you oversee.

89. (　　) Look at the graphic. When did Janet Rossi place the call to Steve Gunt?
    (A) On Monday.
    (B) On Tuesday.
    (C) On Wednesday.
    (D) On Thursday.

From:	Janet Rossi <hr@crestline.com
To:	All Project Managers <Undisclosed recipients>
Re:	BUDGET SEMINAR AGENDA
Date:	October 3 09:11:34 EST

Budget Seminar Agenda
Wednesday, October 4
1:30 p.m.
Conference Room 2A

1:30 p.m.	Keynote speech from Maria Karpova, CEO
1:45 p.m.	Buddy Hield, Outsourcing
2:15 p.m.	Boston Chu, Marketing
2:45 p.m.	Eva Lopez-McGill, Performance Management
3:15 p.m.	————Break and Refreshments————
3:45 p.m.	Steve Gunt, Operations
4:15 p.m.	Closing Notes and Q&A Session with Janet Rossi

GO ON TO THE NEXT PAGE

90. (   ) According to the speaker, what has not changed?
   (A) The workshop topic.
   (B) The project budget.
   (C) The sales goal.
   (D) The meeting location.

91. (   ) Who, most likely, is the message for?
   (A) A computer technician.
   (B) A project manager.
   (C) An accountant.
   (D) A sales clerk.

Questions 92 through 94 _refer to the following speech and agenda._

Thanks, Joe. Folks, thanks for attending today's town hall meeting. As you all know, we're here to address the issue with traffic congestion around the Market Street tunnel. As an experiment, in June we initiated a temporary traffic control program. At that time, we hired three retired police officers to direct traffic in the street leading to the tunnel during the morning and evening rush hours. The trial period was a success, and now that it's over, we have to make a decision. We'd like to hire more people to direct traffic in this area on a permanent basis, but this will require additional funding. So I'd like to introduce Ivan Portensky, city budget director who will explain how we might be able to pay for this new program.

92. (   ) Look at the graphic. Who is the current speaker?
   (A) Joe O'Brien.
   (B) Olivia Collins.
   (C) Ivan Portensky.
   (D) Scott Favreau.

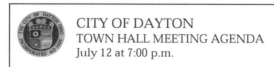

CITY OF DAYTON
TOWN HALL MEETING AGENDA
July 12 at 7:00 p.m.

7:00-7:10   Welcome and introduction   Joe O'Brien, moderator

• Purpose of meeting – Olivia Collins, City of Dayton mayor
• City of Dayton, Office of Budget and Management – Ivan Portensky, city budget director
• Montgomery County Commissioner's Office – Scott Favreau, acting deputy

8:30-9:30   Public comment and open discussion – Joe O'Brien, moderator

---

93. (　　) What did the city do in June?
   (A) Initiate a temporary program.
   (B) Change parking regulations.
   (C) Hold an election.
   (D) Fire three police officers.

94. (　　) What problem is the speaker addressing?
   (A) Scheduling delays.
   (B) Road congestion.
   (C) Budget reductions.
   (D) Street repairs.

Questions 95 through 97 *refer to the following broadcast.*

Good evening, you're listening to the WDJK AM 930 radio news center bringing you local news report for the Cleveland metro area. This weekend, on both Saturday and Sunday, join us at North Beach for the annual sand-sculpture exhibition and contest. Professional sand sculptors from around the world will gather to create the beautiful art. Judges will be present both days and the winner of the best sculpture will be announced on Sunday night. Look out for our own WDJK radio station booth where we'll be serving free hot dogs and soft drinks to keep you and your family refreshed. And now here's Matt for the weather report for this weekend so you can better plan for your day at the beach.

95. (　　) What public event does the speaker describe?
   (A) A sports competition.
   (B) A musical concert.
   (C) A cooking demonstration.
   (D) An art contest.

96. (　　) What will the radio station offer for free?
   (A) T-shirts.
   (B) Wall calendars.
   (C) Food and beverages.
   (D) Upcoming event tickets.

97. (　　) According to the speaker, what will be broadcast next?
   (A) An advertisement.
   (B) A live interview.
   (C) A weather forecast.
   (D) A music performance.

GO ON TO THE NEXT PAGE

Hello. This is Lucy Gonzales with Universal Solutions. I placed an order yesterday for customized business cards and I'd like to make a change. I took a second look at the design I chose and I realized that the red background is too dark, so the company logo isn't showing up clearly. I'd like you to change the background to a standard white instead. And also, please increase the font of my email address by 1 point. Of course, I will pay any additional costs for this. Please call me back on my cell if you have any questions. Thanks.

98. (   ) What does the speaker want to do?
     (A) Hire a designer.
     (B) Change an order.
     (C) Preview an agenda.
     (D) Paint a wall.

99. (   ) What problem does the speaker mention?
     (A) A logo is not clear.
     (B) A shipment is late.
     (C) A printer is broken.
     (D) A name is misspelled.

100. (   ) Look at the graphic. What type of business is Universal Solutions?
     (A) A hardware company.
     (B) A law office.
     (C) An auto repair shop.
     (D) A marketing agency.

UNIVERSAL SOLUTIONS
1234 Delaware Ave., Washington, D.C.
"Branding is our business"

Lucy Gonzales
Senior Media Analyst

Contact: (708) 340-2222 office
Email: l_gonzales@globaloutreach.com

NO TEST MATERIAL ON THIS PAGE

GO ON TO THE NEXT PAGE.

New TOEIC Speaking Test

Question 1: Read a Text Aloud

 **Question 1**

Directions: In this part of the test, you will read aloud the text on the screen. You will have 45 seconds to prepare. Then you will have 45 seconds to read the text aloud.

Traveling long distances with pets can be a chore, especially when they need to relieve themselves. Some smaller pets like lizards or birds can easily be left in their boxes until arrival, because their waste matter is relatively small in volume. However, larger animals such as dogs and cats will need extra care. If you are driving, be sure to let your dog out of the car at a roadside rest stop every 2 or 3 hours so that it can urinate.

PREPARATION TIME
00 : 00 : 45

RESPONSE TIME
00 : 00 : 45

Question 2: Read a Text Aloud

 **Question 2**

Directions: In this part of the test, you will read aloud the text on the screen. You will have 45 seconds to prepare. Then you will have 45 seconds to read the text aloud.

We are currently cruising at an altitude of 35,000 feet. That's about 11 kilometers, for those of you who prefer metric measurements. The weather bureau predicts clear skies between here and Honolulu, so we do not expect any rough patches at all. You will notice that the seat belt sign has been switched off, which means it is now safe to get out of your seats. However, please keep your seatbelt fastened when you are seated. Our flight will take approximately 4 hours. Lunch will be served in about an hour.

PREPARATION TIME
00 : 00 : 45

RESPONSE TIME
00 : 00 : 45

GO ON TO THE NEXT PAGE

Question 3: Describe a Picture

((● 5 ●)) Question 3

Directions: In this part of the test, you will describe the picture on your screen in as much detail as you can. You will have 30 seconds to prepare your response. Then you will have 45 seconds to speak about the picture.

PREPARATION TIME
00 : 00 : 30

RESPONSE TIME
00 : 00 : 45

Question 3: Describe a Picture

答題範例

 **Question 3**

I see a couple holding hands while walking down
a long hallway or corridor.

The lockers on the right suggest this is a school,
and judging from the age of the couple, it's
probably on a college campus.

They could easily be high school students, too.

Anyway, the woman has long dark hair, and the
man has shorter, lighter hair.

They are both wearing jeans; the woman is
wearing a denim jacket, and the man is wearing
a plaid shirt.

Their heads are turned toward each other, as if
they were in conversation, and the man appears
to be smiling.

I can't see the woman's face.

GO ON TO THE NEXT PAGE.

Questions 4-6: Respond to Questions

 **Question 4**

Directions: In this part of the test, you will answer three questions. For each question, begin responding immediately after you hear a beep. No preparation time is provided. You will have 15 seconds to respond to Questions 4 and 5 and 30 seconds to respond to Question 6.

Imagine that an American marketing firm is doing research in your country. You have agreed to participate in a telephone interview about cameras.

Question 4

When buying a camera, what is the most important thing?

Question 5

How often do you take photos with your camera and when?

Question 6

In what way is a digital camera better compared to a traditional, non-digital camera?

Questions 4-6: Respond to Questions

答題範例

 **Question 4**

When buying a camera, what is the most important thing?

Answer

> Well, there are several things to consider when
> buying a camera.
> Certain cameras are better suited for certain types
> of photography.
> Of course, I always consider price and value when
> I'm in the market for a new camera.

 **Question 5**

How often do you take photos with your camera and when?

Answer

> I take photos every so often, usually at social events
> or outings.
> I mainly use my camera to document the memories.
> Other than the camera on my smart phone, I don't
> usually carry a camera with me wherever I go.

GO ON TO THE NEXT PAGE

Questions 4-6: Respond to Questions

 **Question 6**

In what way is a digital camera better compared to a traditional, non-digital camera?

Answer

By far the two biggest advantages of a digital camera are the lack of film, and the amount of storage.

Not using film means you can view the images right away.

Then you can make adjustments if necessary.

Meanwhile, having 16 gigabytes of memory means you can take literally thousands of pictures and not worry about losing the film to bad exposure, or worse, sloppy lighting or poor photography skills.

Digital cameras give you so much more flexibility.

I don't use traditional cameras.

Questions 7-9: Respond to Questions Using Information Provided

 **Question 7**

Directions: In this part of the test, you will answer three questions based on the information provided. You will have 30 seconds to read the information before the questions begin. For each question, begin responding immediately after you hear a beep. No additional preparation time is provided. You will have 15 seconds to respond to Questions 7 and 8 and 30 seconds to respond to Question 9.

Orientation for New ArtCorp Employees

09:00-09:50	Opening address in the Palette auditorium
10:00-10:50	CEO Paul Gordon -"A Brief History of ArtCorp"
11:00-11:50	Video presentation by Thomas Brunn
12:00-13:00	Lunch in the Gallery Cafeteria
13:00-15:00	Group discussion
15:10-16:00	Design demonstration
16:10-16:50	Group tour of the facilities
17:00-18:00	Dinner in the hotel dining room

Good morning, my name is Charlie Hogan, and I am a new employee at ArtCorp. I'm supposed to take part in the orientation program, but I can't find the timetable. Could you answer a few questions for me?

PREPARATION TIME
00 : 00 : 30

Question 7	Question 8	Question 9
RESPONSE TIME	RESPONSE TIME	RESPONSE TIME
00 : 00 : 15	00 : 00 : 15	00 : 00 : 30

GO ON TO THE NEXT PAGE.

Questions 7-9: Respond to Questions Using Information Provided

答題範例

 **Question 7**

I'd like to know what the topic of Paul Gordon's presentation is and what time it starts.

Answer

> Sure.
>
> Mr. Gordon's presentation will be "A Brief History of
>   ArtCorp."
>
> It begins at 10:00 a.m. and concludes at 10:50.

 **Question 8**

Somebody said that there will be a video link to Ai Wei-wei from his studio in London. Is that really happening?

Answer

> Actually,
>
> No.
>
> There will be a video presentation by Thomas Brunn at
>   11:00 a.m., which ends shortly before noon.

Questions 7-9: Respond to Questions Using Information Provided

((◀ 6 ▶)) **Question 9**

I'm afraid I'm going to be late for the orientation because my train doesn't arrive until one o'clock in the afternoon. What will I miss?

Answer

> You'll miss the opening address.
>
> You'll miss Paul Gordon's presentation.
>
> You'll miss the video presentation.
>
> You'll also miss lunch at the Gallery Cafeteria.
>
> After lunch, there are four things left: a group
>   discussion, a product demonstration, and a group
>   tour of the assembly line.
>
> And then we will enjoy our dinner together and have a
>   chance to get to know each other.

GO ON TO THE NEXT PAGE

Question 10: Propose a Solution

 **Question 10**

Directions: In this part of the test, you will be presented with a problem and asked to propose a solution. You will have 30 seconds to prepare. Then you will have 60 seconds to speak. In your response, be sure to show that you recognize the problem, and propose a way of dealing with the problem.

In your response, be sure to

- show that you recognize the caller's problem, and
- propose a way of dealing with the problem.

```
PREPARATION TIME
  00 : 00 : 30
```

```
RESPONSE TIME
  00 : 01 : 00
```

Question 10: Propose a Solution

答題範例

((● 6 ●)) **Question 10**

Voice Message

> Hello, my name is Sonny Sampson, and I'm a Burns Largo account holder. My account number is 045446283. I used an ATM late last night at a truck stop in Santa Fe. The time was most likely around 2:00 a.m. because the clerk said he couldn't sell me any beer. In any case, I must have left my card in the machine. I just took my cash and forgot the transaction record. I know that's stupid of me. I didn't realize it until this morning. Now I'm freaking out about the card. Somebody might have it, and might have worked out my PIN. Please call me back at 655-9332 and let me know what to do. Thank you.

GO ON TO THE NEXT PAGE.

Question 10: Propose a Solution

答題範例

Good morning, Mr. Sampson.

This is Padhma Gupta from Burns Largo.

I've just received your voice message and I am sorry to hear about your situation.

I've gone ahead and cancelled the card based on the account number you gave me.

And I have some good news.

Your ATM card was kept by the machine itself.

For your protection, most ATMs are programmed to keep cards left by customers 30 seconds following a completed transaction.

If your card was not ejected or your PIN re-entered within that time period, the machine kept your card.

I've also checked your transaction history, and it appears your last transaction was that cash withdrawal you described, which took place at 2:04 a.m.

Now, I can go ahead and issue another card to you, but I need you to call me back to confirm some of your security details.

I can be reached at 325-0909 until 5:30 p.m.

Thank you.

Question 11: Express an Opinion

 **Question 11**

Directions: In this part of the test, you will give your opinion about a specific topic. Be sure to say as much as you can in the time allowed. You will have 15 seconds to prepare. Then you will have 60 seconds to speak.

There are some who say that a child's parents can be its best teachers and friends. Others disagree. What do you think and why? Support your opinion with some reasons and examples.

PREPARATION TIME
00 : 00 : 15

RESPONSE TIME
00 : 01 : 00

GO ON TO THE NEXT PAGE

Question 11: Express an Opinion

答題範例

 **Question 11**

I agree that parents can be the best teachers and friends to
their child for the following reasons.

First of all, parents are always close to their children so they
understand them better than anyone.

Second, they love their child without any conditions.

If you understand and love someone, you can teach them and
share feelings, and that makes you a good teacher and friend.

That's why good people have great parents who were their best
teachers and friends.

However, sometimes parents can't be your friend — they have to
be the parent.

Sometimes there are difficult decisions that need to be made, and
certain ground rules to be set and enforced.

When a parent disciplines a child, it needs to serve the purpose
of educating the kid.

At those times, the parent stops being a friend and starts being a
parent, or as the question suggests, a teacher.

As a child matures, they begin to understand that things were
handled in certain ways they didn't appreciate at the time.

However, with hindsight, they realize that their parents always
had their best interests in mind and at heart.

That's a true friend.

NO TEST MATERIAL ON THIS PAGE

GO ON TO THE NEXT PAGE.

New TOEIC Writing Test

Questions 1-5: Write a Sentence Based on a Picture

Question 1

Directions: Write ONE sentence based on the picture using the TWO words or phrases under it. You may change the forms of the words and you may use them in any order.

mask / microscope

Questions 1-5: Write a Sentence Based on a Picture

Question 2

Directions: Write ONE sentence based on the picture using the TWO words or phrases under it. You may change the forms of the words and you may use them in any order.

woman / purchase

GO ON TO THE NEXT PAGE.

Questions 1-5: Write a Sentence Based on a Picture

Question 3

Directions: Write ONE sentence based on the picture using the TWO words or phrases under it. You may change the forms of the words and you may use them in any order.

server / table

Questions 1-5: Write a Sentence Based on a Picture

Question 4

Directions: Write ONE sentence based on the picture using the TWO words or phrases under it. You may change the forms of the words and you may use them in any order.

house / paint

GO ON TO THE NEXT PAGE.

Questions 1-5: Write a Sentence Based on a Picture

Question 5

Directions: Write ONE sentence based on the picture using the TWO words or phrases under it. You may change the forms of the words and you may use them in any order.

vehicle / crowded

Questions 6-7: Respond to a written request

Question 6

Directions: Read the e-mail below.

From: Dylan Murphy <bigmurph@good.com>

To: Carson Jack <west_oak@aol.com>

Sent: Tuesday, May 11

Carson,

I've decided to take you up on the offer to sub-lease your apartment. Hopefully, you haven't found another tenant. Let me know one way or the other.

Thanks,

Dylan

Directions: You've already found another tenant. Write Dylan and tell him the news.

GO ON TO THE NEXT PAGE

Questions 6-7: Respond to a written request

答題範例

Question 6

Dylan,

Sorry, buddy, but you may be too late. Rick Riley has

indicated that he would like the place. He hasn't given me

a deposit yet, but he's promised to do so tomorrow. If the

deal falls through, I'll give you a call.

Be safe and see you soon!

Carson

Questions 6-7: Respond to a written request

Question 7

Directions: Read the e-mail below.

From: Tasha Witherspoon

Sent: Thursday July 3

To: Leona Bernstein

Subject: Schedule change

Leona,

I have a huge favor to ask. I know you said July was the worst time to ask for vacation time, but I was wondering if I could possibly have the week of July 18-25 off? My family is coming in from Pennsylvania and it would be nice to spend as much time with them as possible. If you do me this favor, I promise to make it up to you!

Yours,

Tasha

Directions: You'll give Tasha the time off under TWO conditions. Write her and tell her what they are.

GO ON TO THE NEXT PAGE.

Questions 6-7: Respond to a written request

答題範例

Question 7

Tasha,

Yes, I do recall saying July is the worst time to ask for time off. But, in your case, seeing as how you've been so helpful in the past, I'll offer you a deal. You can have that week off if you do two things for me. First, I need you to work Sunday, July 10, filling in for Brian Kelso. Second, I'll need you to come in an hour early this Friday and help with the set-up.

Do we have a deal?

Leona

Questions 8: Write an opinion essay

Question 8

Directions: Read the question below. You have 30 minutes to plan, write, and revise your essay. Typically, an effective response will contain a minimum of 300 words.

Gun control is one of the most controversial issues in society. Can you imagine a world without guns? Why or why not? Cite examples and reasons to support your opinion.

GO ON TO THE NEXT PAGE

Questions 8: Write an opinion essay

Question 8

Though I'm not a gun owner, I understand the ethical importance of guns and cannot honestly wish for a world without them. I suspect that sentiment will shock many people. Wouldn't any decent person wish for a world without guns? In my view, only someone who doesn't understand violence could wish for such a world. A world without guns is one in which the most aggressive men can do more or less anything they want. It is a world in which a man with a knife can rape and murder a woman in the presence of a dozen witnesses, and none will find the courage to intervene. There have been cases of prison guards (who generally do not carry guns) helplessly standing by as one of their own was stabbed to death by a lone prisoner armed with an improvised blade. The hesitation of bystanders in these situations makes perfect sense—and "diffusion of responsibility" has little to do with it.

A world without guns is a world in which no person can reasonably expect to prevail over more than one determined attacker at a time. Therefore, a world without guns is one in which the advantages of youth, size, strength, aggression, and sheer numbers are almost always decisive. Who could be nostalgic for such a world?

Of course, owning a gun is not a responsibility that everyone should assume. Most guns kept in the home will never be used for self-defense. They are, in fact, more likely to be used by an unstable person to threaten family members or to commit suicide. However, it seems to me that there is nothing irrational about judging oneself to be psychologically stable and fully committed to the safe handling and ethical use of firearms—if, indeed, one is.

Carrying a gun in public, however, entails even greater responsibility than keeping one at home, and in most countries the laws reflect this. Like many gun-control advocates, I have serious concerns about letting ordinary citizens walk around armed. Ordinary altercations can become needlessly deadly in the presence of a weapon. A scuffle that exposes a gun in a person's waistband, for instance, can quickly become a fight to the death—where the first person to get his hands on the weapon may feel justified using it in "self-defense." Most people seem unaware that knives present a similar liability. Therefore, I believe guns are absolutely necessary in society.

TOEIC ANSWER SHEET

REGISTRATION No.

姓 名 / N A M E

LISTENING SECTION

Part 1

No.	ANSWER
	A B C D
1	A B C D
2	A B C D
3	A B C D
4	A B C D
5	A B C D
6	A B C D
7	A B C
8	A B C
9	A B C
10	A B C

Part 2

No.	ANSWER
	A B C D
11	A B C
12	A B C
13	A B C
14	A B C
15	A B C
16	A B C
17	A B C
18	A B C
19	A B C
20	A B C

No.	ANSWER
	A B C D
21	A B C
22	A B C
23	A B C
24	A B C
25	A B C
26	A B C
27	A B C
28	A B C
29	A B C
30	A B C

No.	ANSWER
	A B C D
31	A B C
32	A B C D
33	A B C D
34	A B C D
35	A B C D
36	A B C D
37	A B C D
38	A B C D
39	A B C D
40	A B C D

Part 3

No.	ANSWER
	A B C D
41	A B C D
42	A B C D
43	A B C D
44	A B C D
45	A B C D
46	A B C D
47	A B C D
48	A B C D
49	A B C D
50	A B C D

No.	ANSWER
	A B C D
51	A B C D
52	A B C D
53	A B C D
54	A B C D
55	A B C D
56	A B C D
57	A B C D
58	A B C D
59	A B C D
60	A B C D

No.	ANSWER
	A B C D
61	A B C D
62	A B C D
63	A B C D
64	A B C D
65	A B C D
66	A B C D
67	A B C D
68	A B C D
69	A B C D
70	A B C D

Part 4

No.	ANSWER
	A B C D
71	A B C D
72	A B C D
73	A B C D
74	A B C D
75	A B C D
76	A B C D
77	A B C D
78	A B C D
79	A B C D
80	A B C D

No.	ANSWER
	A B C D
81	A B C D
82	A B C D
83	A B C D
84	A B C D
85	A B C D
86	A B C D
87	A B C D
88	A B C D
89	A B C D
90	A B C D

No.	ANSWER
	A B C D
91	A B C D
92	A B C D
93	A B C D
94	A B C D
95	A B C D
96	A B C D
97	A B C D
98	A B C D
99	A B C D
100	A B C D

READING SECTION

Part 5

No.	ANSWER
	A B C D
101	A B C D
102	A B C D
103	A B C D
104	A B C D
105	A B C D
106	A B C D
107	A B C D
108	A B C D
109	A B C D
110	A B C D

No.	ANSWER
	A B C D
111	A B C D
112	A B C D
113	A B C D
114	A B C D
115	A B C D
116	A B C D
117	A B C D
118	A B C D
119	A B C D
120	A B C D

No.	ANSWER
	A B C D
121	A B C D
122	A B C D
123	A B C D
124	A B C D
125	A B C D
126	A B C D
127	A B C D
128	A B C D
129	A B C D
130	A B C D

Part 6

No.	ANSWER
	A B C D
131	A B C D
132	A B C D
133	A B C D
134	A B C D
135	A B C D
136	A B C D
137	A B C D
138	A B C D
139	A B C D
140	A B C D

Part 7

No.	ANSWER
	A B C D
141	A B C D
142	A B C D
143	A B C D
144	A B C D
145	A B C D
146	A B C D
147	A B C D
148	A B C D
149	A B C D
150	A B C D

No.	ANSWER
	A B C D
151	A B C D
152	A B C D
153	A B C D
154	A B C D
155	A B C D
156	A B C D
157	A B C D
158	A B C D
159	A B C D
160	A B C D

No.	ANSWER
	A B C D
161	A B C D
162	A B C D
163	A B C D
164	A B C D
165	A B C D
166	A B C D
167	A B C D
168	A B C D
169	A B C D
170	A B C D

No.	ANSWER
	A B C D
171	A B C D
172	A B C D
173	A B C D
174	A B C D
175	A B C D
176	A B C D
177	A B C D
178	A B C D
179	A B C D
180	A B C D

No.	ANSWER
	A B C D
181	A B C D
182	A B C D
183	A B C D
184	A B C D
185	A B C D
186	A B C D
187	A B C D
188	A B C D
189	A B C D
190	A B C D

No.	ANSWER
	A B C D
191	A B C D
192	A B C D
193	A B C D
194	A B C D
195	A B C D
196	A B C D
197	A B C D
198	A B C D
199	A B C D
200	A B C D

新制多益全真模擬試題①

主　　　編 / 劉　毅

發 行 所 / 學習出版有限公司　　　☎ (02) 2704-5525

郵 撥 帳 號 / 05127272 學習出版社帳戶

登 記 證 / 局版台業 2179 號

印 刷 所 / 文聯彩色印刷有限公司

台 北 門 市 / 台北市許昌街 10 號 2 F　　☎ (02) 2331-4060

台灣總經銷 / 紅螞蟻圖書有限公司　　☎ (02) 2795-3656

本公司網址　www.learnbook.com.tw

電 子 郵 件　learnbook@learnbook.com.tw

售價：新台幣一百八十元正

2016 年 11 月 1 日初版